COPYRIGHTS

Copyright © 2022 by Andrew Abulu.

THE MONKI PARABOLA novel is part of the Children Animation and Story-Tellers (C.A.S.T.) eBook, Print and Movie series. The C.A.S.T. series are a collection of children, teens and young adults Fantasy, Science Fiction and Adventure stories created by Andrew Abulu and produced by CGI Africa animation studios, Lagos, Nigeria.

To learn more about these Series, visit www.cgiafrica.net

Contact; animator@cgiafrica.net

THE MONKI PARABOLA

POWER AND TERROR IN THE 21ST CENTURY

Five towns, Mogadishu, Ogoni, N'Djamena, Khartoum and Isiro (MONKI) form a virtual Parabola on the African continent.

Someone is trying to open a gateway for something to enter our World.

THE MONKI PARABOLA

The story of Us, our Mythical origin
and our future with Monsters.

Dedicated to

PRINCESS DIANA
For her Selfless LOVE

NELSON MANDELA
For his Personal SACRIFICE

CLIVE (JACK) LEWIS
For his Unusual FAITH

MARTIN LUTHER KING
For his Unshaken HOPE

Long ago, mankind knew the powers that he inherited from the creator. There was a time when the seas were calm and the sky was clear; but the rulers of men put their individual interests before the happiness of the people.

Elders grew thirsty with lust for knowledge without wisdom. Kings sought power without compassion; and so the World lost its soul, then evil became bold and ruled where men once did.

It is in the children that we must once again find our courage. Children who once defeated giants; and young men fought and tamed lions.

The time has now come when the children of man must rediscover the power within, and become whom they were born to be.

Long ago, mankind [...] the powers that h[...] inherited from the creator. T[...] a time when the seas [...] calm and the sky was [...]ar; but the rulers of men [...] their individual intere[...] before the happiness [...] the people.

Elders grew thirsty with lust for knowle[...] without wisdom. Kings sought powe[...] compassion; and so the World lost [...] their evil became bold and ruled where men once did.

It is in the children that we must once a[...] find our courage. Children who once defe[...] giants; and young men fought and tamed [...] lions.

The time has now come when the children [...] man must rediscover the power within, a[...] become whom they were born to be.

CONTENT

PART ONE: A THIN VEIL

CHAPTER 1: Vintage Street

Vintage Street   19

A Crazy Old Man?   26

CHAPTER 2: The Men in Black

Market Street   31

Something is wrong   36

Strange people   38

The Chase   42

CHAPTER 3: A Pandora Box

Alex is dying   49

Meeting a deity   52

This changes everything   59

CHAPTER 4: The Seer

The Monastery   69

The Seer   74

CHAPTER 5: The Meeting Lodge

Meeting Lodge   87

Power and Terror; Forces at Play   90

Call to Arms   99

CONTENT

PART TWO: THE AWAKENING

CHAPTER 6: Journey to Africa

Back to Africa	105
The Journey begins	110
Crossing a Threshold	113
Welcome to Ogoni	116
Meeting the Oracle	118

CHAPTER 7: Waiting for Sàngó

An Ancestry Revealed	125
Recalling a Haunting Memory	131
A Son's Regret	136
The Village Party	139

CHAPTER 8: The God of War

Welcome the Samurai	143
Waking a Sleeping Giant	146
A Declaration of War	153

CHAPTER 9: The History of All Things

The History of All Things	157
Arrival of the Watchers	161
The Great Sin	164

CONTENT

PART THREE: THE GATES OF VIRTUE

CHAPTER 10: Journey to the Lost Worlds

Protecting the Celestial Weapons	171
The Secrets of the Seven Gates	176
Entering the Four Gates to the Lost Worlds	179

CHAPTER 11: Facing Your Fears

The Ancient Leopard Tribe	189
The Three Gates of Time	193
The Realm of the Dragons	199
The Forbidden Garden	203

CHAPTER 12: Second Trial

A Prerogative of Mercy	209
The Value of a Pure Heart	214
The Reward for Peace	217
The Burden of Devotion	222

CHAPTER 13: Final Ordeal

A Final Farewell	227
Glimpse of a Dark Future	231
The Chasm of Dragons	239
A Hero Forged by Fire	243

CHAPTER 14: Paragons of Virtue

Unconditional Love	249
Hope Rekindled	255
The Strength of Faith	260
The Value of Sacrifice	265

CONTENT

PART FOUR: THE WAR OF THE GODS

CHAPTER 15: Heroes Reborn

Only three returns 275

At the Edge of War 278

The Transformation 281

CHAPTER 16: War of the Gods

For God and Mankind 287

An Unexpected Ally 296

Beasts of the Five Beacons 298

A Prophesy Fulfilled 304

A Sad Departure 308

CHAPTER 17: A New Beginning

Ade Returns to Óké-Ífẹ̀ 313

It is not The End 317

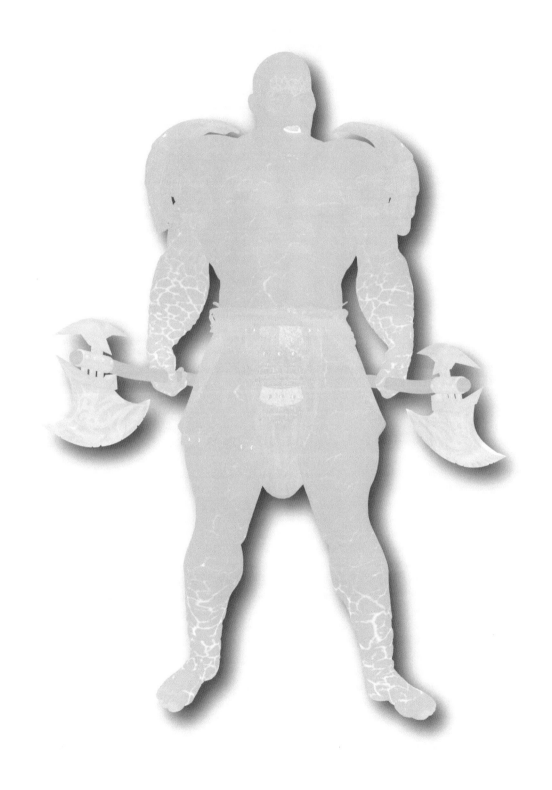

PART ONE:

A THIN VEIL
(ALL IS NOT WELL)

CHAPTER 1: VINTAGE STREET

Vintage Street

It is the first day of the New Year, 2022; the World is still grappling with the menace of the deadly Hydra, the Covid-19 Virus. The pandemic has taken first place in the troubles of the World, beating the worrisome devastation of the environment by the negative effects of Climate Change. With each Covid-19 variant becoming increasingly deadly, the fourth wave of the Pandemic, is being spurned by the Omicron variant, and it is confusing even to the most brilliant scientists of the World, not just because of the super spreading ability but the suspicious mildness of the illness it presents.

Governments all over the World are continuously trying to find a balance between protecting public health and succumbing to public pressure to remove citizen restrictions, which is crippling the global economy and social activities. The dilemma whether or not to continue to shut-down schools is creating a new worry about the immediate and long term negative effects it will have on the already fragile mental state of the children. Small and large scale businesses still grappling with dwindling activities even after receiving various financial bail-out and supports from governments now have to choose between total closure and staff reduction. With new restrictions to social gathering, life around the World is finally grinding to a total halt while the resilient *Generation-Z* youngsters are turning to their ever dependable digital devices and Social media platforms.

With global deaths surpassing the 5 million mark, a new wave of conspiracy theorists are emerging. On one hand some people lean more towards a population reduction theory, purportedly championed by some super rich influential people and organisations engineering the fatal virus and deliberately releasing it into the public with the singular aim to reduce World population. On the other hand, religious fanatics are taking it upon themselves to prepare the World for the impending doomsday, which they believe is long overdue.

Far removed from these scare mongers is a most troubling warning coming from one highly decorated scientist, a man who has worked for over 40 years as senior futurologist at The International Agency for the Protection of Earth and Space (IAPES), London, Prof Timothy Rosi.

Prof Rosi's "New Time Scale" theory revolutionized Space High Velocity Travel Time (SHVTT) with earth time synchronization which is still used till date to calculate precise loss of biological time of Astronauts when they return to earth.

15 years ago Prof Rosi discovered a space rift in Earth's Exosphere. The Exosphere is the very edge of Earth's personal space, so to speak. 1000 kilometers above earth's surface, this layer is the 5th atmosphere which separates Earth from outer space. It's about 10,000 kilometers thick; that's almost the width of Earth itself.

After 3 years of tracking, he discovered that the origin of this unknown rift is located in central Africa. Prof Rosi claims that this phenomenon is unnatural and is being generated by a 4,000 kilometer wide virtual parabolic energy field; he postulates that the phenomenon is man-made.

For several years the Prof has compelled the IAPES to further investigate the source of the rift but his request is always quickly overridden by higher authority.

After several years of rejection by The International Space Congress to make his presentation about his discovery, Prof Rosi finally receives the approval of the Congress to deliver his research paper next week at this year's London conference.

One week passes slowly or so it feels for Prof Rosi as he prepares to leave his house on Vintage Street in the Peckham district of South London where life is still pretty much as it has been since the entire lockdown. Everyone on Vintage Street knows one another, most were born here and their parents as well as grandparents have lived happily amongst one another. The quiet street is now dominated by teens and young adults, who mostly hang out and play outdoor games in small friendly groups. Like many neighbourhoods, Vintage Street has its own undesirable group of rascals trying so hard to be regarded as a tough street gang.

Led by the self-absorbed and attention seeking 22 year old, Chris; the Dark-Shade gang as they prefer to be called always gather in front of his house, cleaning and polishing his trademark yellow Mini Morris car which he hopes will get him some much desired attention from the girls on the street. Sadly for the gang boys, the girls of Vintage Street already have their eyes on the new guy, 20 year old Ade.

Ade, a dark skin African recently moved to the modest neighbourhood with his adopted parents, a missionary English couple who adopted him from Nigeria at the young age of seven and together they have travelled all over Africa, South America and Asia, preaching the Good Word and sometimes volunteering as teachers in those countries. The Dark-Shade boys regularly pick on Ade because most of the girls on the street flirt with him, always trying hard to get his attention, leaving Chris and his gang drooling with envy. Ade keeps to himself but is polite and only bow in appreciation to the advances of the pretty girls of Vintage Street.

At the other end of the street lives a 19 year old biracial beauty, Ibi Smith. Ibi is that neighbourhood chick every guy wants as his girlfriend and every girl wish to be like. Living alone with her English dad who is an oil exploration consultant, Ibi's mother died while giving birth to her. Ibi's parents met in Ogoni, an oil rich town in the Niger Delta of Nigeria, while Ibi's dad was working as an oil-well engineer and her Nigerian mother was a nurse. Devastated by the death of his loving wife, Ibi's dad immediately moved back to England with his new born baby. Over the years, as Ibi became older, her father took up an International oil exploration consultancy job in Kuwait and only visited Ibi in England once or twice every year, but he always sends adequate money for his daughter's upkeep; so Ibi has grown-up emotionally and physically independent and has learnt how to look out for herself.

The other girls of Vintage Street love to be around Ibi not just because of her strong martial arts protection ability but also because she plays the role of a caring mentor who all the girls look up to and one who gets all the boys' attention; but are scared of, especially after the pretty face girl beat-up one of the gang boys.

Living next door to Ibi is Alex; only son of Prof. Rosi. Alex and Ibi have both grown-up together as best pals on Vintage Street. Their extreme close relationship is not very defined. Sometimes, Alex seems to be getting the "be my boyfriend" look from her which only often ends up in a quick peck on his chick. Alex is not one you'll call bold but tries to be "the man" around Ibi whenever trouble is brewing. Let's just say, on his own part, he's Ibi's secret admirer.

Like Ibi, Alex was raised by a single parent. When Alex was five years old, his alcoholic mother moved out, leaving him and his dad; she never came back ever since. Both the young and old Rosi have become inseparable. Though the good Prof is always engrossed with his scientific crank ideas and conspiracy theories, he still manages to get Alex to listen to his ever confusing theories and Alex always pretends to be enthralled. Everyone on the street likes Prof Rosi and he seems to play the role of the good old uncle next door.

And so the morning of Prof Rosi's big presentation is finally here and he is looking confident in his trade mark grey suit and red briefcase as he walks out the house gate towards his bright yellow VW. Alex standing in the doorway whispers their favourite phrase, "Go break a leg".

Alex watches with a worried look on his face as his dad drives off. Ibi walks towards the parting fence between their houses and leaning over the low fence, she puts her hand on Alex's shoulder trying to calm Alex's concerns, "He'll be alright, he does this every year and comes back in one piece". Alex answers his confidant, "Ibi, I don't think this is like the previous years, this time something is different. He seems to be anxious about something, as if there is an urgency of sorts".

Ibi replies, "I admire his tenacity. I wish others were a little like him, you know, stand by what they believe. Your dad is a stubborn but a nice man; he goes for what he wants. You should try that sometime".

Alex looking embarrassed and surprised is left speechless as Ibi walks away with a smirk on her face.

She calls out, "Ah! There are my girls, seems they're trying to get Ade's attention again. I wouldn't blame them though, he looks mysterious and strong".

Alex is jealous and decides not to join the chuckling ladies.

Ibi walks up to the two girls who are trying to start up a conversation with Ade; but as usual, the topless macho ignores the flirty girls. Ibi and the girls continue their chattering. Far off at the other end of the street, the Dark Shade boys can't hide their resentment. The gang boys can barely be heard as they murmur indistinct derogatory remarks about their undisturbed perceived contender. Sensing a build-up of trouble, Ade walks into his house.

A Crazy Old Man?

Later that afternoon, Ade's loud voice draws the attention of the neighbours. He is delivering some groceries to Lucas, who is on a wheelchair. It seems Lucas is up to his usual shenanigans. Lucas used to shop for himself at the market street, just down the road but he is renowned for cheating and sometimes try to avoid paying for whatever he buys. He is also not very popular because he often deliberately owes money for past shopping. Nowadays he asks Ade to do his shopping for him. Ade does personal shopping for many people on the street, particularly the old folks, for a much needed cash because his adopted parents struggle to make ends meet since they are volunteering missionaries who generally work for free.

Like most times, it seems Lucas is up to his old mischievous ways, trying to avoid paying for Ade's services. Ibi rushes to the scene to mediate between the arguing pair. The warring men settle and Ade continues on his delivery rounds.

Just then, Alex's dad's yellow VW pulls up in front of the house.

Prof Rosi walks into his front yard looking half-hearted. Alex and Ibi welcome him and ask how it all went this time. The downcast Prof sadly answers, "I need a drink".

Alex replied, "That bad, eh?"

He tells Ibi, "I need to be with him". Alex goes into the house with his dad.

Inside the house, Prof Rosi gets a drink for himself and sinks into his favourite chair. Turning to Alex, he complains, "The fools! Who will act if they do nothing? They are the World's best scientists but they prefer to bury their bald heads in their outdated books. Even after I told them that I have the exact coordinates of the five towns in Africa that make up the massive virtual parabola, they still weren't interested in sending a research team to the locations".

He continues angrily, "And that mediocre chairman of the governing board, all he was interested in was my file. What impertinence, asking me to submit my research findings and they'll find time to peruse it. Peruse it, he said. That man hasn't done any research work that anyone can remember, yet he is put in charge. I can't believe I've wasted the past seven years trying to convince the congress to support my research. The way they even spoke to me makes me wonder if they think I'm crazy".

Alex, speaking sarcastically, "Well, don't worry dad, it runs in the family".

Prof Rosi replies, "At least yours has a name, insomnia".

Alex cuts in, "I don't suffer from insomnia. I'm just scared to sleep sometimes. I get these dreams and they seem so real. In the dreams I find myself lost in a strange World of Dragons and I can't seem to find my way out".

Alex snaps out of his own brief daydream and continues, "Anyway, we are not talking about me. Don't you think it's high time you gave up on your wild conspiracy theory? After all, the science congress is the body of experts and they should know better".

Alex's dad is frustrated; he remarks, "I just don't understand. I presented undisputable proof that the parabolic rift in our Earth's atmosphere is not a space rift like I thought but a Dimensional Rift, and from the readings I'm getting at the office lab, it has become traversable".

Alex looking confused asks, "And that is bad I presume?"

Prof Rosi continues, sounding even firmer and more worried, "That means things can pass through".

Alex getting more inquisitive, "Things like, …?"

His dad sighs; and now speaking in a concerned manner, he explains, "Matter and extraterrestrial beings can cross from one end into the other. I know that sounds implausible, but that's the problem. We know very little about what is beyond our physical World and I was hoping that the learned scientists would at least be curious to know what and maybe who is responsible for this phenomenon. If you ask me, the rift is too perfect to be some kind of random cosmic event. I have reasons to believe it is man-made or at least made by some form of highly intelligent being".

Alex sounding frustrated, "So we are talking aliens now? Come on dad, can you hear yourself?

Alex continues, "Maybe that's why mom left".

There is a brief silence then Alex walks to his dad, "I'm sorry dad. I shouldn't have said that. Mom's leaving has nothing to do with your crazy ideas", Alex smiles.

Prof Rosi looks up from his sitting position towards Alex, feeling let down, he laments, "Not you too! You don't understand, my gut feeling is that something really bad is about to happen to our World".

Alex casually answers, "Something bad is already happening, Covid-19 is killing millions of innocent people, that is real. This…portal thing isn't".

The dad feeling helpless, succumbs, "You are probably right, what can one old man do? Maybe I'm actually getting cracked up".

Alex, trying to cheer his dad, "No you are not. I'm proud of you. You stand up for what you believe".

His dad cuts in, "And you should too. Just tell her how you feel before you lose her to..."

Alex shocked and embarrassed, "What…? Lose who?"

Prof Rosi replies, "Ibi of course. You two have been more than friends since you were kids. It's obvious you are in love with her. Just tell her how you feel".

Alex, still embarrassed, "How did we go from aliens to…and…don't you even say that. Anyway, I believe things that are meant to be should happen naturally".

His dad replies, "Well son, I'm afraid, in this modern World, they don't. People can't see what is in front of them, at least not anymore".

They both sigh and hug each other. Alex looking into his dad's eyes, "All will be fine dad, you'll see".

Alex gets up and picks up a shopping bag, he changes the topic, "Anyway, we are running short on groceries; I'll just hurry to get a few things. Will you be okay?"

The dad assures Alex, "You go on, I'll be alright".

As Alex walks out the door, he turns around and with a curious expression, he asks, "But why do so many bad things always seem to happen all at the same time?"

His dad replies, "My son, there are things we know and there are things we do not know".

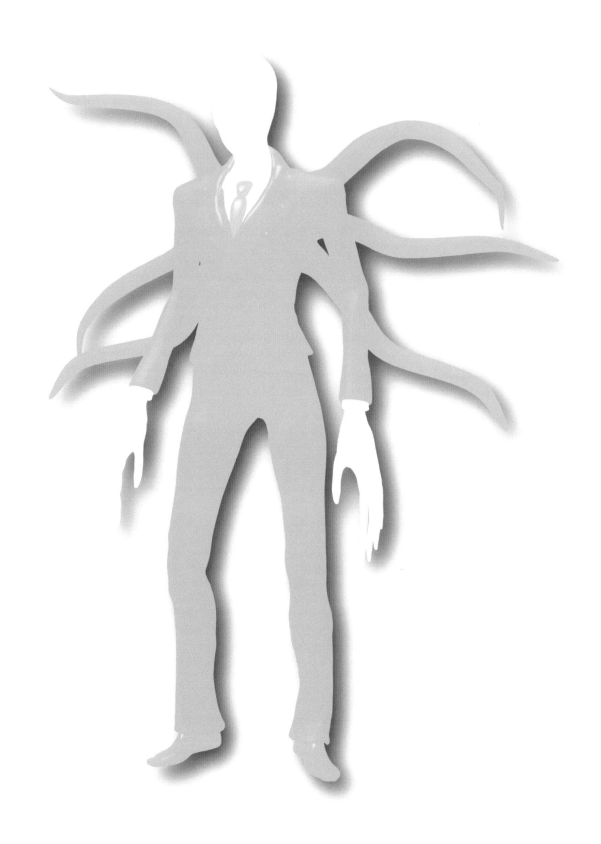

CHAPTER 2: THE MEN IN BLACK

Market Street

At the market street, Ibi and Alex are spotted by some of Ibi's young fans from Vintage Street. The four excited teens drag Ibi to a clothing stall for tips on which clothes to buy to look tough but trendy like her. Ibi is amused; she joins them in their youthful pick and drop shopping routine. Alex feels left out and as usual decides to just wait it out as a by stander.

Their fun time is disrupted by some commotion from a nearby stall. It's the troublesome Dark shade gang harassing Ade, but ignoring the troublesome lot, Ade continues with his shopping.

Seeing Ade completely surrounded, Ibi yells from afar as she runs towards the bullies. Ade stands his ground and is ready to fight back. Alex tries to stop Ibi from getting involved, fearing that they are outnumbered by the ruffians and also hoping that the gang could help scare his one competitor off his girl.

Ibi breaks free from Alex and rushes into the middle of the fracas and tries to stop the impending brawl. Seeing the unfolding scenario, the four teen girls run off while Alex looks on at a distance.

With a sarcastic smile, gang leader, Chris strokes Ibi's hair and threatening her, "Hey beautiful, you shouldn't get into fights that aren't yours, you know, you could get your pretty face scratched".

Ibi swiftly twists the gang leader's outreaching arm and bends his fingers backwards, causing him to shriek in pain. Alex now feeling more confident, stands behind Ibi hopping up and down cheering Ibi's move and yelling, "You boys be careful how you talk to the Kung-Fu expert, or she'll kick your sorry asses!"

Two gang members grab Ibi's arms and hold her down. Chris, the gang leader moves closer to Ibi, threatening further, "I could kick your pretty ass you know, but I don't hit chicks".

The Other gang members shouted, "Yeah, we don't hit delicate chicks".

Another member of the gang boys pushes Ade, teasing him, "Hey errand boy, I want you to run to my house and fetch my stick".

Ade politely replies, "I'm sorry I don't do personal errands. I only do groceries and my fee is…".

The fat gang boy bursts into an irritating laughter as he nudges Ade with his finger, "So the mute talks".

He continues his pestering, "Now that I've loosened your tongue, tell us where the Reverends picked you from".

Ade calmly obliges, "I was adopted by my noble parents, the Reverends Brown".

A gang member interrupts, "Adoption is good. Tarzan was adopted, by Apes".

All the gang members burst into a mocking laughter. Ade shakes his head and turns away to continue his shopping but the biggest gang member steps even closer to Ade and whispers to Ade, "Hey Tarzan boy, have you learned the ropes?

He pulls a sharp blade from his jacket and steps dangerously close to Ade, as he continues his whispering, "We can teach you how to be…"

Before he completes his sentence, Ade spins around and with an unprecedented agility, he snatches the knife from the aggressor and presses the blade on the throat of the perplexed gang boy. Ibi breaks free from the gang boys and screams to Ade, "No! Stop, let him go; they are not worth it".

Meanwhile Alex standing behind Ibi, stunned by Ade's move and scared that something horrible might happen next, keeps murmuring to himself, "That's not good, that's not good…"

Ade pushes the now terrified gang boy away from himself and calmly narrates a brief background of himself. I was adopted at the age of twelve from my village in South West Nigeria after surviving in the harsh streets in the company of my *Area-Boys* for five years".

He looks sternly towards the gang leader and continues, "Everyone called me cold-hearted. They said I was inhumane".

The gang leader arrogantly asks, "And why did they say that?"

Ade looked around and at the faces of all those present, then answers, "When I was about seven, maybe; there was a famine in my village and people were dying of hunger, no food and no firewood even.

So, I let my dog help. I loved my dog, it was very loyal to me, slept mostly in my arms but I let him serve the people".

Speaking from behind the lot, Alex asks, with a shaky voice, "So it fetched firewood from the forest?"

Ade looking into Alex frightened eyes, responds, "No, I gave it to my street pals as meat".

Alex, feeling disgusted and almost hyperventilating exclaims, "Oh, Sugar! You are indeed inhumane".

Ade explains further, "I was just trying to help my beloved dog… you know, end his misery of hunger".

There is an immediate deafening silence, and then Ade drops the knife and picks up his scattered bag of fruits.

Alex now trying to be friends with the tough Ade as he walks towards him, "We should stick together and they'll never bother us again".

Ade ignores Alex and just walks away. Ibi calls to Ade, "Please wait".

Ade turns around, and with a sort of gratifying look at Ibi, bows slightly and without saying a word, the stern face loner walks away.

Something is wrong

Alex and Ibi get back to Vintage Street and find a gathering of people, a fire trucks and an ambulance in front of Alex's house. A dark smoke is emanating from his house. He runs towards his house shouting, "Dad!"

Ibi runs after him. Fire fighters can still be seen putting out a fire in Alex's house and his dad lying on a stretcher with emergency services nurses attending to him. Alex pushes through the Police barrier and crowd as he keeps yelling, "Dad!" He gets to his dad, hysterical and shouts, "What happened, are you okay?"

Calmly his dad reassures him, "I'm fine son, I'm fine". His dad pulls the still shaken Alex close to himself and mutters, "I told you they'll come after me. They are after my findings".

The old man hands over a file folder he has been clenching close to his chest and continues in a shaky voice, "Take this file, it contains the coordinates of all five towns where the terrestrial gamma flashes are being generated and when exactly critical mass of the Dimensional Rift will be attained. They must be stopped".

Alex, confused and worried asks again, "What are you talking about? There is nobody after you, I'm sure it was just a regular house fire caused a gas leak or electrical fault. You need to get a good rest and…"

"Listen!" his dad cuts in, "There is a lot more I have not told you or anyone but you must keep the file secret until we know who to trust".

Ibi pushes her way through the crowd to the Prof's side and is immediately grabbed by the old man who begs her, "Please look after him, they will be after him now, keep him safe; you're all he's got now".

Ibi assures the Prof, "Don't worry, he'll be fine, and you are a tough old fighter, it will take more than a barbeque flame to beat you. Alex will stay at my place until you get back, you just focus on getting better quickly".

Just then Ibi's eye catches a glimpse of the same Rover jeep she saw at the market street, this time parked at the end of Vintage Street. As the ambulance drives away with Alex's dad, Ibi pulls Alex aside, warning, "Come quickly, let's get inside, something is not right here".

As the crowd disperses, Alex and Ibi go inside Ibi's house next door. Inside the house Ibi asks, "Did you notice that White Rover SUV packed at the end of the street?"

Alex still unsettled and confused by all the commotion replies, "What SUV? I don't understand what is going on, I'm worried. I'm beginning to think that my dad may be hallucinating. What if the fire was actually started by him" What if he is actually going around the bend?"

Ibi interrupts and queries Alex, "I don't think your dad is going crazy. Why will you even think that? You are all he's got. He needs your love and support now more than ever".

Alex cowers into himself and sobs as he explains, "I don't know what to think or do. All this is too much for me".

Ibi moves close to Alex and pulls him close into her tight embrace, "All will be well, I'm here for you".

Alex raises his head up, looking into Ibi's eyes with a subtle gaze, he steals a quick kiss to her unsuspecting lips. Ibi quickly pulls away from Alex, looking away and walking straight to a couch, she sits down without saying a word. Alex not knowing how to follow-up his unanticipated expression of love, just walks to Ibi and without saying a word, sits beside her.

Strange People

The following morning Ibi and Alex get up early and without any change of clothes or breakfast, hurry out of the house and head for the hospital to check-up on Alex's dad. Still unsure if they're being watched, Ibi lead the way through a back alley to the Market Street bus-station.

As the duo emerges at the empty market corner, they are confronted by the same Rover SUV.

Three stern looking men dressed in black suits step out the car and march towards them.

One of the stout men pulls out a menacing looking knife as he walks towards Ibi. Alex catches a glimpse of the knife and with a terrifying voice screams, "Look Ibi, he has a knife". What do you want from us, you obviously must be after the wrong people, we are just two nobodies".

Ibi steps in front of Alex, facing the advancing men, as she puts up her fists.

As the knife wielding strongman raises his sharp pointed blade, Alex pushed Ibi aside, away from the attacker and gets stabbed in the process.

He lets out a shrieking scream of pain, "he stabbed me. The brute stabbed me!"

Suddenly they hear the screeching sound of car tyres. A Mini Minor pulls up in front of them and Ade leaps out of the car yells, "Get in fast".

As Ibi rushes to get into the car from the left side giving Alex a shorter distance to enter the car from the right side, she sees Ade pushing an already slouching Alex back, preventing him from getting into the car, saying, "Not you, feeble boy".

Ibi yells at Ade, "What are you doing? He has been stabbed. I'm not leaving without him".

Ade hisses and orders Alex, "Alright, come on get in…and be quick".

The Chase

The three narrowly escape the hefty men as they get into the car and zoom off.

Ibi yells and nags at Ade, "What's wrong with you? Were you seriously going to leave him with those armed thugs?"

Ade calmly responds, as he continues his car maneuvering, "It's not him they're after. It's you".

Ibi is shocked and asks, "What do you mean it's me they're after? I don't understand!"

Ade continues his stunt driving, trying to out-run the pursuing Rover jeep.

With Alex moaning at the back seat, Ibi continues her bickering, "And, really? This car of all cars? The Dark Shade gang Mini? Couldn't you get something bigger or at least faster?"

Ade takes a side fleeting look at Ibi, and replies a badgering Ibi, "A thank you should suffice".

Ade takes a left turn, heading out of town, causing another outburst from Ibi, "Where are you going? You missed the turn to the Hospital".

Ade still in his unperturbed demeanor answers, "We are not going to the Hospital. The Hospital cannot save him. That was not an ordinary blade and those are not ordinary people"

Ibi questions further as she turns around to check on the groaning Alex at the back seat every few seconds, "What are you talking about. Do you know those people…or whatever they are?"

Ade still driving quite fast and rough keeps uttering his instructions, "Hang-on". "Brace yourself". "They're catching-up". "Better start praying, this car can't go any faster".

Ibi with a frown, responds, "You don't say".

Between his moaning and crying, Alex pleads, "Can you two just stop complaining, I'm the stabbed one here. You need to get me to the Hospital".

Ade turns into an abandoned factory site and mutters out confidently, "Finally!" He continues talking to himself, "A little help here will be appreciated".

Ibi wondering who Ade is talking to, asks, "Who are you talking to?"

Far ahead they see a parked construction Scoop Loader ahead.

The driverless vehicle starts-up and moves on its own towards the edge of the road. As the two speeding cars get close, the Scoop Loader's bucket is lowered and rams across the street on to the oncoming cars, narrowly missing Ade's car.

Crashing into the SUV and causing the Jeep to somersault.

Ade heaves a sigh of relief as he and his company make a clean getaway.

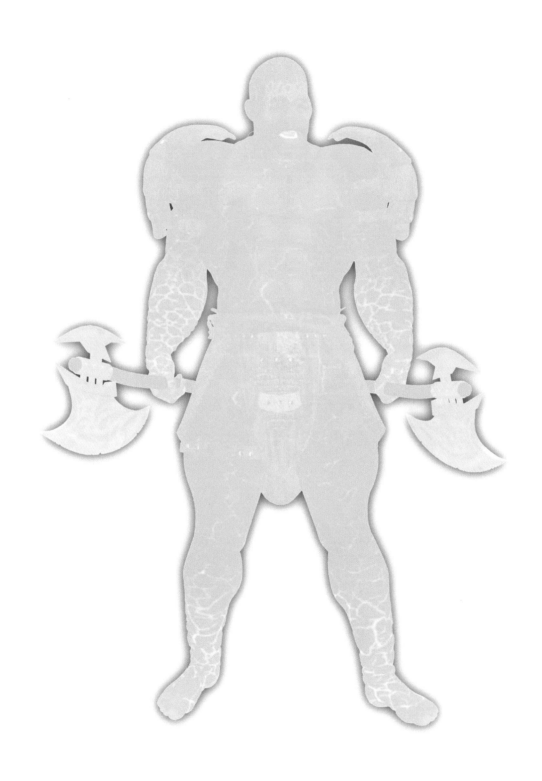

CHAPTER 3: A PANDORA BOX

Alex is dying

arrowly escaping the Scoop Loader's bucket, Ade drives through a series of abandoned

warehouses. Ibi confused about what just happened yells out to Ade, "Did you see that?" She continues in

her shock, "That Loader didn't have any driver. It just drove itself".

Ade ignores Ibi's questions and just concentrates in his rough driving, meandering through narrow spaces

and tight corners. Ibi looks over to Alex at the back seat; Alex seems to have passed out. She tries to wake

him up, calling out his name but not getting any reaction from her wounded friend. Ibi starts to cry, querying

Ade, "He's dying, I told you we should have taken him to the hospital; he is losing consciousness".

Ade takes a quick glance at Alex and continuing in his maneuvering, he assures Ibi, "He'll be okay".

Ade slams the brakes just before crashing into a large rusty grey gate; jumping out from his driver seat,

beckons on Ibi, "Hurry, help me get him inside".

Confused but obliging, Ibi helps Ade carry her very weak friend into the dusty abandoned warehouse. Ibi,

furious and impatient, asks Ade, "Now what?"

Ade confidently replies, "Now we wait".

Alex opens his eyes, groaning and in a frail voice, complains, "I don't feel so good". Continuing in his weak voice, "I think they're after my dad's notes. It seems they're the ones my dad warned me about".

Ade cuts in, "It's not you they're after it's Ibi".

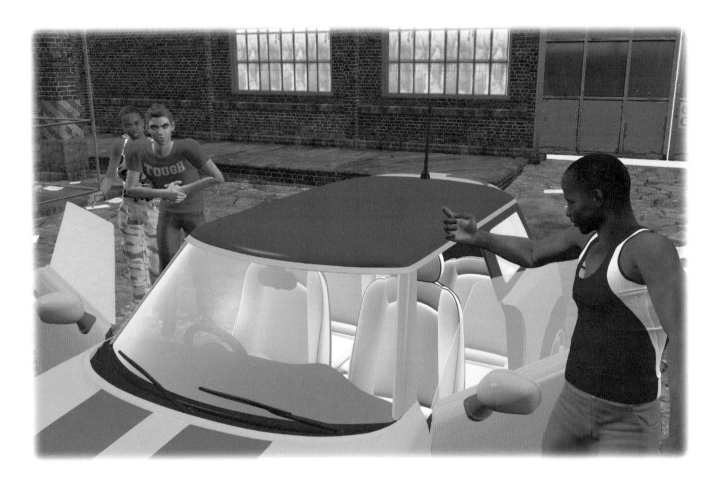

Stunned, Ibi asks, "Me? What will they want with me, I'm nobody. I'm sure you must be mistaking".

Ade walks away from the inquisitive pair, looking around the abandoned warehouse, he answers Ibi, "You are the key".

Ibi charges towards Ade, "What are you talking about, what key… key to what?"

Ade turns around and confronts Ibi, "It seems you are or have some kind of power or thing that will save the World from some impending disaster".

Ibi tries to enquire further but Ade cuts in again, "Don't ask me, I just do as I'm told, I don't even know if I believe what…"

Alex is surprised and looks back and forth between Ade and Ibi but his pain gets worse and he soon slumps over the Mini.

Amidst the questions and arguments with Ade, Ibi's attention is drawn to a weakening Alex. She rushes to Alex and yelled at Ade, "Look here mister I-don't-care, can't you see that he needs urgent medical help?" She insists, "Now get into this tin-can and let's get out of here and go straight to a hospital".

Ade walks back to the car and looking at the fading wounded Alex, speaks empathetically, "I'm afraid no doctor can save him.

Those men who attacked you were not ordinary people and Alex was stabbed with a Mabuki reaper". Ibi now getting concerned asks, "A Mabu what?"

Ade sighs as he explains further, "A Mabuki reaper is not just an ordinary object or knife but an entity. It is a demon entity or evil human who can take on the form of an ancient weapon. They have existed and were first used in tribal wars many centuries ago. The demon spirit of the weapon entraps and feeds on the spirit of the victim".

Meeting a Deity

Ibi, fuming with anger and disbelief, stomps around the Mini Car to confront Ade but Ade shushes Ibi and whispers, "Quiet". They hear several footsteps outside the closed grey gate. The gate slides open and the same group of men in black confidently walk towards the helpless three.

With red glowing eyes, the four vicious men charge towards the frightened trio. Suddenly from the dark shadows of the warehouse comes a thunderous roar and explosion.

Several bursts of lightning shoot out from behind the even more frightened youngsters, knocking the four strange men tumbling backwards to the ground.

A fierce giant dressed in tribal warrior attire emerges. With his huge strides, he stomps angrily towards the four fallen intruders. Raising two fiery axes in his flaming hands he utters several strange words, generating deafening thunder and lightning.

The four men in suit rise up and begin to morph into faceless skinny creatures, each having wavy tentacles protruding from their backs. As they walk towards the advancing giant, they growl and float above the ground.

Ibi kneels over the already slumped Alex while Ade seems to be addressing the raging giant and pointing at the four approaching ghoul like beings.

The defending giant leaps over the car and lands in the middle of the shape shifting skinny-men, generating a vibration that reverberates across the entire warehouse.

The warrior giant spins around with his axes stretching wide and knocking two of the floating shape shifters to the ground. His flaming kick also bashes a third skinny-man far off. The forth ghoul shrieks as it jumps towards the wild giant. Swinging his two axes across each other, the angry giant forms a scissors-like slash chopping the fourth villain in half. The four humanoids disintegrate and evaporate into thin air.

The four fiends dissolve and evaporate, leaving no trace of their bodies.

The giant turns around and walks straight to Ibi and speaks to her in a strange language but Ibi doesn't understand and just stares at the towering giant. Ade speaks to the giant in Yoruba; the language of the Yoruba tribe from West Africa; telling him to speak in English so that the others can understand.

Still maintaining his stern look, the giant turns to Ibi and with an echoing voice calls her name, "Ibinabo bearer of good tidings". The Giant continues, "Indeed, you are as was foretold, the brave one, a warrior at heart".

Ibi interrupts, "I don't understand, how do you know my name and who are you?"

Ibi turns to Ade, looking confused, she asks, "Did you know about all this?"

The giant leans over Ibi and speaking more calmly to Ibi, he introduces himself, "I am Ṣàngó, Orisha of thunder and lightning, warrior of the ancient Yoruba Empire, third Alaafin, of the Oyo Kingdom, son of Oranmiyan and descendant of Odùduwà, the Divine King".

Ibi interrupts again, "Sounds really nice but my friend here is dying, I need to get him to a hospital unless from all what you have told me, you have some portion or something to heal him".

Ṣàngó kneels next to Alex who is now unconscious and murmurs strange incantations and sings a melancholic tribal song. As Ṣàngó continues singing, the sadness in the melody feels the air and tears seem to form in Ibi's eyes. A glow of yellow aura starts to form around Alex. Gradually Alex opens his eyes and feels well again. He calls to Ibi, "Hey, I feel great".

Then suddenly Alex notices that Ibi does not pay any attention to him and he also notices that he is actually floating a good six feet off the ground. Looking down Alex sees his own body lying on the floor.

He shouts in panic, "What the fudge?", but no one hears his yelling.

He thinks to himself, "Wait a minute, I'm I dead? I can hear my own heartbeat. Is this how it feels like?"

He thinks to himself again, "Death is not so cool after all, it is confusing and scary, and it feels very lonely".

His usual logical thinking kicks in, "Oh, I'm not dead, after all. I can see Ibi, Ade and who the fudge is this monstrous hulk-like giant?"

Ṣàngó continues his incantations and melancholic singing.

Alex gets even more confused and panics; thinking to himself, "I can see myself. I mean, I can see my own freaking self; down there. It's like I am floating, hovering over my body. Am I going to be one of those ghosts hanging around trying to make contact with my girlfriend through one fake medium? Anyway, I saw that old movie, Ghost; you know, the one with that crazy old scamming medium, who later found out she could actually hear ghosts. No! I'm getting ahead of myself; this must be some kind of trick. I never trusted that Ade boy. I didn't like the way he looked at Ibi. Yes, I know I sound a little jealous or okay, maybe more than a little jealous".

Ibi starts to cry, telling Ṣàngó, "Please save him. He's all I've got, I love him, please save him".

Ade moves across to console Ibi as she continues sobbing.

Alex for a brief moment smiles saying to himself, "Yes! I knew it, she loves me; and you Ade don't you get your filthy paws on my girl".

Alex tries to float back down towards his body but it is futile, in ghost land, there doesn't seem to be gravity when you need it. Gradually, Alex feels everything going dark, he struggles to keep himself awake but he soon loses consciousness but this time, he is fainting in ghost World.

Suddenly, Alex is awoken by a sharp pain in his abdomen. He groans, "My stomach!"

Ibi jump unto her feet and tries to hug the friendly giant but quickly recollects herself.

Ade walks to Alex, still lying on the ground and greets him, "Welcome back, for a moment I thought we lost you".

Alex looks around for Ibi, expecting a romantic hug or something but instead gets a scolding from her, "That was just a little knife scratch and you gave us a scare".

Alex feeling that this is chance to get his girl, confidently confronts Ibi, "I heard you in my unconscious state, you said you loved me, so why don't you just admit it? Come on give me a kiss, it's the least I deserve".

Ibi put up her usual tomboy personality with a straight face, she replies the lover boy, "Not on your life".

Alex gets up and hurries behind Ibi as she walks to Ṣàngó. He stutters as he tries to call her back, "But, but".

This Changes Everything

Ibi ignores Alex's beckoning and walks straight to Şàngó. She clasps their hands in front of her and courtesies to the giant, thanking him for protecting them from the attack of the evil creatures and saving Alex's life. Şàngó in return, nods in appreciation. Şàngó explains who the Skinnymen were. He tells his curious guests that the shape shifting ghouls are actually spies and dark infantry of a viler demon, Brutus Demonicus, also known as Nybras, who is the head of the order of demons and whose only objective is to prepare for the final destruction of mankind. Brutus is one of the original rebel angels and loyal servant of the Prince of all evil, Lucifer himself.

He explains that Ade, Alex and Ibi's coming together is no chance meeting but ordained by fate and they must now accept the responsibility and task of forming a resistance force which has been long foretold to be the ones that will defeat the angel of darkness.

Ade cuts in, interrupting Ṣàngó's speech and demands that he be set free from any more duties, insisting that his role in the so called divine task is already done. He asserts that his initial obligation from Ṣàngó to deliver Ibi has been fulfilled and so he is not going to be part of another quest.

Ibi snaps in, "What obligation, so mean all this while you've been stalking me pretending to be a friendly neighbour? You're pathetic".

She then turns to Ṣàngó and asks why he wanted her brought to him. Ṣàngó gives a deep sigh, then he explains to the group that a great impending doom is inevitable and they have been chosen to prevent it.

He continues, "Long ago, mankind knew the powers that he inherited from the Creator. There was a time when the seas were calm and the sky was clear; but the rulers of men put their individual interests before the happiness of the people. Elders grew thirsty with lust for knowledge without wisdom. Kings sought power without compassion; and so the World lost its soul, then evil became bold and ruled where men once did. It is in the children that we must once again find our courage. Children who once defeated giants; and young men fought and tamed lions. The time has now come when the children of man must rediscover the power within, and become whom they were born to be".

He tells them that there lies within each of them a unique ability and a role each must play in the task ahead and if they refuse or fail in the quest, then evil shall be let loose upon all of the land and the Devil and his demons will reign and have dominion over the World.

He then leads the sobering group, "Come with me, let us go, there is little time and there is much to tell you and lots of preparations to be made".

Ṣàngó takes his new team to an open yard at the back of the warehouse outside where he reveals to them details of the enemy's plans.

Ṣàngó narrates how several Watcher Angels were sent by the Creator Himself to guide humans and keep them from immoral and wicked ways and also to help them grow in wisdom and knowledge. This task the celestial Watchers did but over time the Watchers witnessed mankind procreating and growing in numbers and they also began to lust after the finest of the women, wishing also to procreate; for never could Angels bear offspring. Discovering that is it the Earth that brings forth, they soon understood that being on Earth they also could procreate. Thus the heavenly angels began to seduce women from the human tribes and so began to lose their own holiness. They began to teach humankind various forbidden celestial skills and secrets, including the art of magic and war. The Watchers and their demigod children born from their acts of fornication; Nephilim, as they were called, soon grew in numbers and began to lead large groups of men and women through long distances to new lands, founding large and powerful kingdoms.

Then the Lord sent a powerful archangel to bind the devil and most of his associates and God then caused a great flood to cleanse the lands. Most of the unclean were destroyed but some of the demons of Satan survived as well as some of the Nephilim children of the Watchers.

Ṣàngó tells his bewildered guests that he also is a product of the descendants of the survived Nephilim. While he and his defenders have enormous strength and great knowledge, they have not inherited the likeness and authority of the Creator. Ṣàngó also discloses that Brutus has led four other vile demons over the ages to setup powerful kingdoms and secretly rule such kingdoms, seducing and corrupting the minds of men.

Now Brutus Demonicus, being the leader of the dark side on Earth is preparing to open a gateway between the dark realm and our World for his master, Satan and his horde of devils to take over the World.

Ṣàngó further reveals that he and several Nephilim descendants have fought Brutus and other foul demons over the ages but they continue to lose the battles. Now, Brutus Demonicus is gathering the five surviving demon warlords to set up five beacons in five towns in the cradle-land of mankind, the heart of Africa. Now he Ṣàngó and a few other protectors must unite the chosen children of man and it is they who will defeat the evil which is about to unfold.

After hearing all what Ṣàngó narrated, Ade gets angry and asks why God Himself, with all His powers just ignores all the enemy's deeds and does nothing to stop any of it.

Turning to the two young men and Ibi, Ṣàngó replies, "God created humans in His likeness and they have inherited His essence giving humans godlike abilities to fulfil their primary role of developing, caring and protecting the World, therefore the Father cannot interfere directly else mankind will lose the authority and dominion over all that he has created for them. He only intervenes to lift people up when they falter and He is always available when people ask for help. Sadly, the World has fallen asleep and forgotten who they are, where they come from and the reason why they were created".

Ṣàngó continues, "Now we must all unite in arms and spirit to confront our common enemy by rediscovering that lost connection with one another and the Universe. That is the only way we can hope to defeat this potent foe whose plans are now set and ready to destroy the World".

Ibi asks Ṣàngó, "How did that Brutus monster and other evil creatures survive the great flood, do they have amphibious characteristics or could they have flown out of the Earth and returned after the flood cleared? I don't see how they could have escaped their intended destruction".

Ṣàngó pauses for a moment then replies, "There are things we know and there are things we do not know".

Ṣàngó continues, "And that's not all. We only have a couple of days before the final phase of the enemy's plan is initiated. You three must go immediately to The Jesuit Abbey in St. Andrews. There you will meet The Seer; he is the wise one. He will tell you what you must do and help you with all that you will need".

Alex exclaims, "What! That's in Scotland, in fact, far along the West Coast of Scotland country-side. That's a ten hour drive".

Pointing to the Mini, he expresses his frustration even more, "And in that, it will take us a whole day".

Supporting Alex's doubts, Ibi sarcastically murmurs, "That's if it gets there at all".

Ade chips in boldly, "I can make it in three hours".

Alex hisses as he objects, "Who made you the leader, no way I'm sitting at the back this time".

Ade turns to Ṣàngó and asks sarcastically, "That's if you have a Ferrari".

Ibi and Alex both burst into laughter, pointing at and mocking Ade, "Where are you going to get a fast car in this old abandoned warehouse, talk less of a Ferrari".

Ṣàngó cuts into their chortle, "Ahem! I just might have a Ferrari packed just down over there". He points to the far end of the large junkyard.

Ṣàngó walks his new team to the edge of the yard. They spot a red Ferrari and immediately race to the bright red sports car.

Ade gets to the car first, opens the driver's side door and smiles as he nods repeatedly, saying, "Now that's what I'm talking about".

Ibi interrogates the giant, "Aren't you coming with us?" She continues her query, "You started this, you can't just send us off to some unknown Monastery, to some mysterious stranger!"

Şàngó explains, "I have been in deep hibernation for centuries. My body and weapons are still trying to adapt to this realm and era. I need some time to recover my full strength. You go ahead; I will surely catch-up with you".

The three excited rookies get into the dazzling race car as Şàngó, now looking pensive, bids them farewell, saying, "We are now in uncharted territory".

Ade puts the pedal on the metal and the tiny red beast responds with the gentle sound of a throaty rumble then suddenly explodes with its characteristic thundering roar, reverberating in the entire surrounding.

Looking at the speedometer needle go from zero to sixty in three seconds, Ade puts up a grin of satisfaction.

Noticing that Ade is in a pleasant mood for once, Ibi dares to ask, "By the way, Ade, how did you meet Ṣàngó?"

Ade's smile slowly morphed into a contemplative expression, then turning to Ibi, the tough guy narrates, "It was my first week in Vintage Street; and not knowing my way around the shopping district, I got on my bike to explore the neighbourhood. I had barely ridden through a few streets when I noticed a yellow Mini Minor tailing me."

Ibi interjects with a sigh, saying, "the Dark Shade gang".

Ade responds in the affirmative and continues, "I lost them in a crowded streets for a while but missed my way, emerging on to the highway. They found me and ran me over. I was hurt but I still tried to defend myself. They pulled out knives while the leader, Chris, the leader watched in amusement. I tripped and fell making it easy for the five thugs to surround me. I thought I was a goner for sure when suddenly; there was a loud blast of thunder and lightning. From within the misty cloud that engulfed us all, emerged a flaming giant. The gang scampered, tumbling over one another. As for me, I was too hurt to run, yet somehow I was not afraid. It seemed like we were communicating telepathically. After the gang boys ran off, the flames of the giant subsided, revealing the magnificence of the creature. He called my name and spoke to me in my native language, Yoruba; telling me not to be afraid. He took me inside that abandoned warehouse and miraculously healed my wounds. He then narrated the same tale of doom, you both just heard and told me of the prophesy and that you, Ibi was essential to his plan to save mankind. He made me promise to bring you to him and my role would be done. I tried to get close to you, hoping to win your trust and maybe convince you to meet with him but it seems fate had some other plans and the rest is what you know already".

The three new friends continue their drive; with each one asking long-harboured questions and many times they laugh and ask more questions. Each of the three take turns to drive the sports car, competing on mastery of driving and other motor skills.

CHAPTER 4: THE SEER

The Monastery

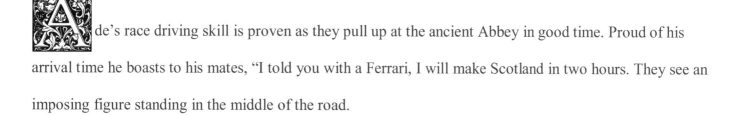de's race driving skill is proven as they pull up at the ancient Abbey in good time. Proud of his arrival time he boasts to his mates, "I told you with a Ferrari, I will make Scotland in two hours. They see an imposing figure standing in the middle of the road.

The three travelers stare at the Monk-like bearded man for a moment, wondering what is next.

They step out of the car then notice something quite odd. Ade yells, "What the…"

His other travel mates are also gobsmacked as they see that they were actually stepping out of the same unimpressive Mini Minor car they drove in to the warehouse and not a Ferrari at all; and not even a red one at that.

Forgetting the Monk character the three youngsters freeze in amazement.

The Seer welcomes the still dazzled youngsters. knowing why they're stunned, he smiles as he tells the three team members that Ṣàngó loves to play these illusion games; telling them that it's Ṣàngó's little game he calls seeing is believing. It is a lesson he tries to teach most people he meets that there is more to see than what is in front of you.

The Seer explains that Ṣàngó has anyways been this way since they both met when the giant was a stubborn little giant kid. Trying to calm his new guests, the Seer explains further, "Ṣàngó never really had the opportunity to be a real kid; he was raised and treated as a future King right from birth. That is what some of us have to sacrifice, being what we are".

Ibi inquires, "You speak as if you are one of the demigod children but you look normal, I mean human, just like us.

The Seer answers, "Yes, I am a first generation Nephilim born with the gift of my father, who was also a seer. I inherited his ability to read the stars and interpret the constellations but did not inherit his physical form. He wasn't a giant like many others; he was a *Therianthrope*, a mix form, part man, part beast; like a Mermaid, or in his own case, a Merman. He wasn't a fish though. He was part man and part bull".

Alex burst in, "A Minotaur!"

The Seer smiles in surprise, "Yes, exactly; he had the body of a man with the head and tail of a bull. The wise Minotaur, as he was called, he was big and strong, wise too, very wise".

Gazing up to the sky, the Seer continues his tale, bringing back fond memories, "I took my mother's human form but inherited my father's gift of clairvoyance; the ability to read the stars and sometimes even able to influence their movements".

Looking at the three travelers, he asserted, "You too can do that you know, you have more powers than you know. All humans do, the Creator gave you much of His essence, and you must learn how to connect with the Universe. It takes a strong belief and something else which most people would rather not do".

The Seer beckons to his guests ushering them to come inside the monastery with him but still standing in amazement, they all asked simultaneously, as if planned, "Do what?"

The Host turns around and replies, "Conquer you. Your biggest enemy is your ego. People build huge statues of themselves and place it in front their own path, blocking their own way, making it difficult for them to move towards their destiny".

Speaking thoughtfully, the Seer continues, "There are two beings in everyone, you and yourself. So I ask, who are you, and what do you do about yourself? You cannot teach a man whose cup is full, and not even of water; may I add, but of himself. When someone's mind is full of nothing, you can't get something into it anymore. You must always control yourself".

The Seer smiles, trying to soften the mood, "Come now, you all must be tired and hungry".

Ade, still dumbfounded by Ṣàngó's illusion car spell, murmurs to himself as he stands steering at the Mini Minor. Alex and Ibi laugh at the previously confident Ade as they follow their host into the decaying wooden gates of the ancient monastery.

The Seer

After eating a much appreciated hot meal, the host leaves the trio to some alone time to let the weary travelers settle in.

While Ibi and Alex play their silly games, Ade spends his alone time pondering about the entire unfolding events. The Seer eventually walks into the Monastery courtyard and breaks the tranquil of the young guests.

 He sits down on a stone bench under the shade of a tree and invites his guests to sit with him. He tells the now relax trio, "There is a lot to tell you but I'm afraid, there is very little time and so much to do".

Continuing, he says, "There are things we know, and there things we do not know".

Alex interrupts the old man, "Oh, not you too!".

The Seer continues, "Yes, I'm sure someone must have said that to you. That's because it's true. Indeed what I'm about to tell you now may be too much for young people like you to understand, but it must be said and you must listen very carefully".

Alex enquires further, "Are you some sort of Gandalf?"

The Seer, asks, "A who?"

Alex asks further, "You know, a wise wizard with supernatural powers, whose job is to teach us magical stuff and lead us on our heroes' journey".

The Wise old man shakes his head in disagreement, "I am one of many helpers; Keepers, as we decided to call ourselves; we are a group of new watchers assigned to protect mankind from the evil that still lurks in the World. We have protected the World for many generations of man, ever since the original watchers became corrupted and also brought corruption to the peoples of the World. We recite the following words as a reminder of past mistakes and also hope for the future..."

"...Long ago, mankind knew the powers that he inherited from the Creator. There was a time when the seas were calm and the sky was clear; but the rulers of men put their individual interests before the happiness of the people. Elders grew thirsty with lust for knowledge without wisdom. Kings sought power without compassion; and so the World lost its soul, then evil became bold and ruled where men once did. It is in the children that we must once again find our courage. Children who once defeated giants; and young men fought and tamed lions. The time has now come when the children of man must rediscover the power within, and become whom they were born to be".

Ibi thoughtfully responds, "Yes, we have been told that already by Ṣàngó, after the attack in the warehouse in London".

The Seer nods and continues, "The World faces an imminent danger once again from a group of demons from a prehistoric era; led by Brutus Demonicus; the ruler of hell on earth, whose true name is **Belial**.

Brutus leads four ancient hell servants;

Beelzebub, Lord of the fliers

Dagon, Prince of the Depths

Moloch, consumer of infants' souls,

and *Chemosh* the destroyer.

For many Millennia, we the new watchers have dreaded the predicted unification of these beasts and now, I'm afraid, they have truly been awakened. Each of these foul beasts has taken position at five towns in the heart of the birth place of man, Africa. Mogadishu; the capital city of Somalia on the coast of the Indian Ocean. Ogoni; an oil rich town in the Niger Delta of Nigeria. N'djamena; capital of Chad lying at the East bank of the Chari River. Khartoum; capital of Sudan, the largest country of the African continent is located just south of the confluence of the Blue and White Nile Rivers and Isiro; chosen to be the focus of the virtual gigantic parabola, it is located near the Uele River; a tributary of the Ubangi in the Democratic Republic of Congo. Together, these five towns form the MONKI parabola.

When activated, the virtual parabola will generate an intense rift which will then open an interdimensional gateway between the realm of hell and our World, allowing billions of hell's creatures to invade and desecrate all that is good on Earth".

With his eyes betraying his fear, Alex asks, "You mean Ragnarok, the twilight of the gods; the ultimate battle between demon giants and the champions of mankind; the ultimate battle and final destruction of the World?"

The Seer, looking confused asks, "Ragnar what, I don't know what that is, but you get the general picture. Yes, it's the war to end all wars; one which began in the heavens but must now be determined here on earth by mortal men".

A deafening silence follows, and then Ibi soberly asks, "What can three ordinary mortals like us do to stop this calamity? I think you need to get a whole army of supernatural giants, like Ṣàngó to fight this war of yours".

Ade also concurs, "You have the wrong team here. I think we have just wasted our time and yours coming all the way here".

Alex dumbfounded, murmurs to himself, "I can't believe my dad has been right all these years. He has been trying to warn us all but no one believed him, not even me, his son".

Ibi tries to console Alex, "Don't beat yourself, even after hearing all these; I'm still trying to get my head around it all".

The Seer turns to each of the young team mates and continues his incredible tale, "The MONKI Parabola is not their first attempt to open a supernatural portal. In the 1970s, due to the worsening world energy crisis in the World, experts were uncertain about the continuous availability of the commodity. World petroleum demand was increasing far more than reserves. Projections were that the World would run out of crude oil by 2030 and natural gas by 2050. On the other hand, environmentalists were worried that burning large amounts of fossil fuels was creating by-product gases that were accumulating in the atmosphere and trapping excessive heat energy from the Sun causing what is now known as the Greenhouse effect.

They feared that it might lead to an increase in global temperatures, which might in turn disrupt global weather patterns and create other environmental problems; even Nuclear energy, which was thought to be an alternative to fossil fuels, generated radioactive wastes with enormous health hazards and disposal problems.

Not long after various power-generating projects were proposed as alternatives to petroleum and other fossil fuels. After two decades of intensive research, hundreds of renewable energy options were proposed. One project which stood out as the most renewable and clean option was proposed by energy revolutionary giant, Megatron Energy Company. The company pointed out that since energy storage for night-time use was the main problem in all solar power systems; the solution was to find a way to generate another corresponding solar energy at night. To produce this night energy, Megatron Energy Company proposed that creating a *Night Sun* was the only solution; an outer Sun located behind the Earth in our solar system. Their plan was to initiate the fusion of the planet Jupiter. In 1995, spacecraft, Ulysses, launched in 1990, by NASA and the European agency passed by the poles of our Sun and gave a clear insight as to its nature. It was revealed that the Sun's structure was formed when gravitational energy released by the collapsing gas heating the core and creating the nuclear burning of hydrogen into Helium. Earlier spacecraft, Voyager 1 and 2 launched by NASA and reaching Jupiter in 1979 revealed that over 80% of its atmosphere is molecular hydrogen with Helium forming most of the remainder. This was a composition similar to that of our Sun. Megatron also noted that Jupiter is Located in fifth position in our solar system, just behind the earth, making Jupiter perfect for the cosmic experiment. In March 1993, Comet Shoemaker-Levy was discovered near Jupiter and having brushed the giant planet had been transformed into over a dozen warheads and was projected to be making for a direct hit into the planet in late July 1994. Megatron proposed launching additional Nuclear Warheads into Jupiter to boost the expected explosion of the gaseous giant planet and thus cause the fusion of its hydrogen into Helium and releasing energy thereby giving birth to a young sun.

Due to global outcry and some resistance from us, the Guardians, Megatron's project was aborted and the expected death of Jupiter was prevented. If the Megatron had achieved the creation of a double Sun, they would have had enough cosmic energy to generate an interdimensional portal".

The Seer continues, "Following the failure of his secret Jupiter-Sun fusion plan, Brutus knows that the MONKI Parabola rift is his last opportunity to bring his master into this World before their imminent judgment. He will stop at nothing to see it through".

Ade thinks for a moment and then suggests, "Why don't we just offer them a sacrifice; Alex here should do. It's not like he is useful to anyone".

Ade turns to Alex and then giggles. Alex, reacting to Ade's ridiculous suggestion, snaps, "Well, what do you know? The stiff can crack a joke".

Ade replies sarcastically, "Joke? That wasn't a joke…"

Ibi tries to intervene but Alex gears up and confronts Ade, "You see, I knew you never liked me. You tried to leave me back in London after I was stabbed by those men in black and now you're trying to get rid of me; or maybe you are just intimidated by my…".

Ade responding with a mocking laughter, "By your what? Oh please…"

Ibi cuts in, "Guys! That is enough. Why do guys always fight whenever there's a girl around?"

The two warring guys look at each other embarrassingly. The Seer, holding up both hands to each guy's face, tries to diffuse the tension, "Okay, that was refreshing and good; at least you two are now communicating. Now it's time for you three to put away your petty differences and come together to form a team and hopefully become the heroes that you were foretold to be".

Alex in astonishment asks the old man, "You mean we will become heroes of the World?"

The Seer disagrees, "No! True, the path will be laid out before you, but it is you who must decide whether or not to take that path".

Ade also questions the wise old man, "So, you don't even know if we will succeed in this task?"

The Seer affirms, "No, I do not. No one can predict the future. All that I can tell you are the possibilities of an action, not the outcome of the action or event".

The wise old man add, "For our struggle is not against flesh and blood, but against the rulers, against the powers, against the world forces of this darkness, against the spiritual forces of wickedness in the heavenly places".

Alex sighs, "That's it then, I'm out. I'm not going to risk my life on such a dangerous and unpredictable journey without an assurance of success".

Ibi reminds the nagging friend, "You were already dead, remember. At least you know what it feels like to be dead".

The Seer reassures the hesitant young man, "Death is a path we all must take. It is a part of life, you must never be afraid to walk that path. It is the only way you can be united with the Creator; when your time comes, you must embrace it, which is why you must always try to do what you were appointed to do in this life".

The Seer continues, "This night Brutus and his horde of dark servants will converge at their annual meeting manor in London. There each servant will step before the fierce demon to give account of their stewardship as leader of the industry where he or she has been planted. Those who fail to achieve their set mission will face his swift wrath".

Ade boldly proposes that the team should storm the meeting place and kill Brutus. He suggests, "All we need is bait. When the flesh eating demon starts devouring his prey; Brutus, like all predators, will become enthralled by his feast and so will become vulnerable and that will be a perfect time for us to attack and kill the big bad boss".

Ade then turns and faces Alex. Alex is horrified by Ade's gory suggestion and accuses the impetuous lad, "You are unbelievable. Do you really hate me that much or just want to get rid of me so that you can have Ibi all to yourself?"

Ade quickly counters Alex, "I didn't mention your name, did I? And you know what? She is not my type and who told you I want her anyway?"

Alex deciding to fully confront Ade, follows up, "Common, mister wise guy, you are just using that cheap reverse psychology, pretending not to be interested in Ibi hoping that will make her curious and want you. That's a bit archaic don't you think?

Ibi shakes her head as she protests, "I can't believe both of you! Will you both get your testosterone under control and focus on the task at hand?"

The furious girl emphasizes further, "And besides, I'm not interested in either of you. You are both childish and just for the record, neither of you are my type… and I am not some sort of prize you can both fight over".

The Seer is amused at the three warring team mates and concludes, "I think we have our leader here. You two boys better behave else you will unleash the fire in her".

He concludes, "In any case, your bold plan to storm the meeting place is not only suicidal but completely foolish".

Pointing to Ade, "It seems you are full of anger. You have a lot hatred bottled up in you. Whatever has happened to us must not define us. You cannot fight an external enemy when you are already fighting a war within yourself."

As Ade becomes more sober, Ibi asks the old man, "So, what's your plan?"

The Seer stretches his arms over the anxious three and proclaims, "Ade; I see your heritage in the stars; you come from a long line of great Kings, and so you must be just and kind always. Alexander, you are called, the defender of the people, and so you must protect the weak. Ibinabo; I see that you are a bearer of good news; you shall bring the light that'll extinguish the growing darkness that threatens to engulf the World. You three must put aside your differences and become heroes of the World. To defeat the enemy you must know the enemy. You have much to learn and so much preparation to be made before you'll be ready to face what no one has ever faced.

CHAPTER 5: THE MEETING LODGE

Meeting Lodge

After the altercations of Ade, Alex and Ibi, the Seer pulls this new team to sit close beside him, then talking in a whisper, he speaks to them firmly, "Now understand this, it has already begun. At exactly midnight tonight, a continuous line of luxury cars will pull-up in front of an old English mansion; the secret headquarters of the dark congregation".

Once every year on the day when the Sun, Earth, and Moon are in alignment, a Supermoon is formed. It is a day the Moon comes closest to the Earth, making the Moon appear big and exerting a strong effect on all things on Earth; causing strange and insane human and animal behavior. It is on this special full Moon day each year that the disciples of Satan on Earth from all around the World gather to give account to their master, Brutus here in England.

At exactly midnight, a line of glittering Rolls Royce stream in to an ancient manor; each carrying a high ranking member of the various orders of men and women. This order of men and women who have pledged absolute loyalty to their master; come from far and wide; all being revered World leaders; Presidents, Kings and many influential players from all aspects of global trade. They have infiltrated and violated every major industry, especially the music, fashion and movie industries, corrupting what was once good and pure; selling their foul ideas as new and trending ways, particularly to unsuspecting children and young adults. One by one, these prominent people arrive in affluence, magnificence and glamour. It is believed that not all who come are human and not all can be seen with the naked eye.

The Seer continues, "Over the years, our spies have identified many well respected high ranking members of society who come to give account of their successes in influencing the World towards the ways of darkness. We also now know the various orders and the powers each wield. Most importantly, we are certain who their demon master is and the present stage of their mission".

The ancient Palladian palace looks unsuspectingly simple, surrounded by a large garden with a wide flight of steps, which seems to elevate the visitor from the present to an ancient realm. Inside the triple height entrance hall is a range of green marble pillars, each sculptured with the face a prehistoric fiend. A huge black oak double swing door catches the immediate attention of the entrants; guarded on either side by a hooded live gargoyle-looking creature clenching a fiery red pitch fork, is the entrance to the main hall. Above the doorway is an insignia of the ruling demon Belial; whose name is also Brutus Demonicus; around the emblem is the lodge's motto, written from right to left in Enochian script, which translates in English to "He is coming".

The black door opens revealing a congregation of formally dressed men and women whose faces are covered with scary looking masks. The attendees form two rows of disciples waiting to take their turn in front of their master. A thick white smog shrouds the mysterious boss, who seats on a throne formed of human skulls and his dark red skin only partially seen. Standing guard around the throne are several skinny-men with their protruding tentacles and a beastly stout man-like being dangling a long hairy tail.

Also moving across the throne, like a pacing royal guard is a monstrous creature with the head and upper body of a dragon and a lower body of a serpent; floating two feet above the ground. Finally, lying on the floor in front of the throne is the master's pet hellhound, staring at all the lined-up devotees with its green peering eyes.

Power and Terror; Forces at Play

One by one each leader of industry steps forward, they remove their mask to reveal their identity and bare their soul before their master, Brutus; the leader of hell's five powerful demons on Earth. These men and women, who have been placed in the high chairs of our World, state their report before the intolerant master.

First to be summoned is Lady Cecilia Duncan, President of the *European Children Publishers Company,*

ECPC. Lady Cecilia removes her plague mask and bows before the throne.

In her baritone voice, she reports, "Oh great lord and master of our sacred order, in my capacity as the head of largest publisher of children's learning and entertainment books, we have, in the last one year produced over five thousand picture books influencing the young generation to keep secrets from their parents and manipulate their guardians to stop believing in those outdated tale of the Nazarene. We are now setting-up a free global portal where all children can congregate freely without the restrictions of their primitive parents".

There is low pitch roar from behind the fog, signaling the approval of the demon master.

Next to present his report before the terrifying Lord is Dr. Frederick Anderson, Chief Executive of *Fast-Grow Chemical Company*.

Despite his imposing muscular physique; the head of the largest American agrochemical and biotechnology corporation, trembles as he makes his presentation, "My Lord, our range of genetically engineered crops has drastically reduced fertility rate and human population. We had a few minor huddles in North America from some trouble makers in Congress but we have rebranded the company and have received approval from several countries for our new product which will genetically modify human embryos and produce wide spread Immunosuppression. Our next phase will be to discretely release our novel Severe Acute Respiratory Syndrome virus, causing a devastating global epidemic, such as the World has never seen".

He gets the approval of the master.

Then a sharp click-clack sound of high heels echo in the large hall as the Chairperson of Europe's largest fashion collection, *Étoile*; steps in front of the white smog. She removes her death mask, exposing the flat facial effect of Madame Lina DuPont.

Like the others before her, she states her clandestine agenda which also earns her the approval of the roaring beast. Following the fashion queen is an upcoming American Hip hop rapper and songwriter who is being groomed by the Grand Lodge for the next generation music revolution. He proposes how he is working to organize massive initiations, misleading the unwary youth into pledging their souls during concerts, to the dark side, by making them believe it's just a mock ritual and just part of the show and celebrations.

Transnational illicit weapons dealer, Prince Wahab; notorious for selling biological reactive agents to terrorists gets a scare from the demon Lord, who not impressed by the criminal's report; growls in protests, "Prince Wahab, I have only received one thousand souls, yet you promised me more, much more!".

The villain trembles as he replies, "My Lord, ten thousand more are already set to be delivered; my bandits are raiding the farming village of Kasala in West Africa, as we speak".

Brutus roars even loader, "Go! I'm becoming impatient". The desert Prince bows as he recedes, answering, "Yes, my Lord".

CEO of streaming giant; *CaptureNet TV*; producers and distributors of Children and Young Adults content; Mark Luckers, looks confident as he assures his master, "By next quarter, our fantasy preschool series, *Journey to Hades* will introduce the, *Bet your soul*, challenge which will give young children the freedom to be initiated into our *Hell's Angels program*".

Several other high ranking industry players take their turn to state their organizations' successes in influencing the larger World.

The Demon Lord giving his endorsement to all those who had just made their presentation, is interrupted by a late comer; the flamboyant preacher; Apostle Benjamin. The Apostle dressed in his symbolic white suit strolls leisurely into the hall and arrogantly addresses the beclouded monster.

Suddenly in a coarse and thunderous voice that feels the hall, Demonicus roars, "Benjamin!".

Shivering and stuttering, the Apostle answers, "My Lord".

Demonicus yelling in a deafening growling voice continues, "I hear you have been boasting, telling your congregation that you have supreme powers. I hear too that you have acquired three more private jets".

Apostle Benjamin struggles to explain, "My Lord, it's all to win more followers for you".

The angry demon gets up from his throne and leaning forward, his huge size and terrifying form is shown for the first time to his faithfuls. In a most fearsome rage, the demon Lord yells, "Followers?"

"…of what use are followers to me? I have thousands of demons followers, strong and obedient…"

"…what I need are their souls, to feast upon them and claim victory over the light!"

Apostle Benjamin's legs wobble as he observes the serpent dragon floating behind him. He stutters as he speaks, "Ye…yes, my Lord. I promise, I will give you millions of souls…please give me more time, my Lord".

Demonicus turns around back to his throne, giving the Apostle a moment's ease. In a lightning swift move, the floating serpent violently coils around the unsuspecting Apostle, like a python ready for a death squeeze and yanks him mysteriously through the solid marble floor, leaving only his arms and head protruding above the hard floor. Immediately, the master's hellhound gets up and walks slowly towards the stuck Apostle, like a predator stalking its prey.

The apostle pleads for mercy in desperation as he struggles to get free from his frozen entanglement, but the fallen preacher soon realizes that he'll get no mercy from the kingdom of darkness.

The black ferocious hound pounces on the Apostle, locking its huge jaws on the human's head and snapping it right off. As the hellhound devours the severed head, the ghost of the apostle can be seen floating away from his body. The confused and terrified spirit of the apostle is then drawn towards the red demon lord.

Brutus Demonicus takes a deep breath and inhales the helpless spirit of the dead Apostle.

Call to Arms

The Seer explains to the shocked young heroes that the ultimate mission the dark congregation is to corrupt all that is pure and good in this World and make mockery of Heaven and the Creator. The wise old man expounds further that this they have done for a millennia but now they know that their end is near, so they are desperate because for all their successes in the corruption of the World, they still have not be able to break through the god-spirit in the first born of God, in the cradle continent and so the bond between man and his Creator remains unbroken; nonetheless the five fearsome demons have found a way to open a gateway into our World for all hell to invade. This will give access to billions of vile spirit a direct entrance to our World. Each of the five controls a beacon located in five towns that form the MONKI parabola. In seven days, three planets, Saturn, Mars, and Venus will line up with Jupiter, creating a Celestial phenomenon and power that can be harnessed. At a precise moment, each of those five beacons of the parabola will be activated and will generate an unseen wave which will connect the five towns of Mogadishu, Ogoni, N'djamena, Khartoum and Isiro creating a parabolic energy that will unlock the secret gateway between dimensions and time. The prince of Darkness himself will lead a billion demons into our World. If this happens, all hell will break loose; literarily on Earth, and Lucifer will reign physically in this World. In turn Heaven will respond with what has been prophesied for generations as the Rapture. The few good people will be called into Heaven and the remaining people will be deprived of the opportunity to atone. They will be judged with the Devil and it's horde of imps and will be condemned to a void of nothingness till the end of time.

As the Seer continues his narration of the unthinkable gloomy end of mankind, Ade springs to his feet, shouting, "No, no, no! We have to stop them!"

The old man takes a deep breath then tells the young team that they must travel immediately to the International airport in Aberdeen where they'll meet someone who has already made all the travel arrangements for the trio to leave for the oil rich city of Port-Harcourt, in Nigeria, from where they will be taken to the ancient town of Ogoni. There all they must do will be revealed to them.

The wise old man sees fear in the eyes Alex; turning to each of the young heroes, he speaks, "You must put away the fear of the unknown. You must stop thinking that an extraordinary or strange phenomenon is too supernatural for you to confront, for there is no greater supernatural being than a human being, created in the image and likeness of the omnipotent Creator Himself. It is this god-seed planted in man that the enemy seeks to destroy before he can conquer mankind; so man must never give-up that which gives him authority over all creation".

The Seer sends forth the trio with his final words of encouragement, "The light shines in the darkness, and the darkness has not overcome it. The enemy always seeks to deem the hope of man; his main weapon is to make you believe that you cannot win; for if you take away hope from a man, you take away his will to continue to fight. Remember this, there is always hope. Now you three heroes of mankind go with the hope of us all. It is time to end the reign of the prince of darkness".

Then the old man adds, "Now one last thing. Come with me; this should lift your spirit and get you fast ahead".

He leads the group to the back of the monastery where a bright red Ferrari is packed.

They are speechless with excitement and with a satisfying smile, the old man hands the car key to Ade.

Ade taps Alex on the shoulder and proudly announces, "Now, my brother, get in and let me fly you to the moon".

Ade revs the car loudly, disturbing the quietness of Monastery with the thundering roar of the Turbocharged racer; then he unleashes all 700 horsepower of the sports car as they zoom away.

PART TWO:

THE AWAKENING

CHAPTER 6: JOURNEY TO AFRICA

Back to Africa

The excitement of driving in the super-fast Ferrari is lost in the shadow of the impending doom. The three young heroes speak little to one another. They arrive just in time to meet their contact at the Aberdeen Airport checks, who quickly checks them into the six -hour flight. Inside the aircraft Ibi's childhood memories rush back when she realizes that she'll finally meet her mother's side of the family. Ade looking quite pensive also thinks about stepping on his biological fatherland from which he had to flee as a child. Alex sleeps through most of the flight only to wake up to ask for food. Ibi breaks the silence asking, "Guys, what do you think about all of these?"

Alex replies, "Which part exactly are you talking about? Is it the disappearing car act, the flaming giant or the fact that we are being sent to do battle with a soul gulping prehistoric demon Lord?"

Ade responds more thoughtfully, "For me, it's strange that I have to face a fate I've tried all my life to avoid, even accept as real. Now that same destiny has found me and it seems I have no opinion in the matter".

Alex tries to cheer his team mates, "Guys, think of it as a vacation; an all-expenses paid vacation to soak-up some much needed tropical Sun".

Ibi, not motivated by Alex's enthusiasm answers, "You don't get it! This is no walk in the park, neither is it some Hollywood movie. It's worse that watching a ghost movie, because we are in it!"

Bursting Alex's bubble, he laments, "Why do you always have to be too serious. You just snapped the thin thread of courage I had left. Now, I'm already seeing things".

The scared lad looks around the aircraft cabin as if he is expecting something bizarre to happen.

The six hours pass quickly and the plane touches down at the Port-Harcourt City International Airport in Nigeria.

All three hundred and fifty passengers take their sweet time to remove their hand luggage from the overhead stowage bin, making the disembarking time seem longer than the entire flight time. Ade feeling restless, complains, "Why did we have to sit all the way at the back of the damn aircraft?"

Alex for the first time agreeing with his new friend whines, "Yeah, I thought we were the celebrities on board, I mean, not after arriving at the tarmac in a Ferrari!"

Ade cuts-in, "Patience, my man, patience. Don't be like the ungrateful Tortoise".

Alex wondering, asks, "What Tortoise?"

Ade becomes philosophical, "It's an African proverb. It's about a Tortoise found at the edge of a desert, dehydrated and half alive. Instead of the animal to be grateful for being saved, it yells at his saviours for being too slow at picking it up. They decide to leave the unappreciative reptile to its fate and the rude Tortoise dies of thirst. So the people learnt the important lesson of patience".

Ibi butts in, "So your African persona is kicking in already?"

The aisle clears eventually and the three eager travelers step out of the aircraft to experience the warm heat from the bright African Sunshine.

As they walk down the aircraft stairs, they spot a neatly dressed mature man beckoning to them on the tarmac.

The host welcomes the exhausted travelers, "Welcome to Port-Harcourt. My name is Makato; I will be your host and guide throughout your stay here".

Alex is surprised to find an Asian as their guide, he can't hide his surprise, so he probes their guide, "Err… how come you, a Chinese is our guide, here in Africa?"

Makato smiles and replies, "Firstly, I am Japanese, not Chinese and secondly I work here in Port-Harcourt". Ibi gets into the driver's side of the car and notices that the steering wheel is on the left side. She slides to the passenger side and with a mocking expression she looks behind to her two companions at the back seat and they all burst into laughter.

Alex cynically remarks, "We are not in Kansas anymore".

They all simultaneously respond, "We are in Pandora".

The laughter continues as the car leaves the airport.

Makato smiles and interrupting the giggling trio, he resumes his introduction, "My name is Makato Kishimoto but most people call me Mark. I am a specialist geologist for an international company working on the proposed River State government Ring Bridge connecting over twenty individual Islands. I've been in Port-Harcourt all my life; I was born here. My father was the pioneer seismologist of the company. I welcome you once again to the garden city of Port-Harcourt".

Ibi gets right to the point, "I believe you know why we are here, so where are you taking us?"

Makato does not hesitate either, "I like that; you are a person who doesn't waste her time".

Alex doesn't agree with the urgency. He objects, "Now hold on a minute. I'm not going to travel all the way to the famous land of Afro beat and … and not have some fun".

Ade gently disagree with Alex, "I understand your excitement; actually it's tempting not to want to see the fun side of the Port-Harcourt and indeed other cities in Nigeria, especially the Mega city of Lagos, but I must agree with Ibi on this; we are here to save the World. Let's do that first and then we can check out the local colour, if you know what I mean".

Ibi terrifying stare at the two guys quickly shuts them up.

Makato smiles and shakes his head states firmly, "Ibi is right; work comes before pleasure".

Their guide continues, "I am a member of the *Earth Guardians Order* and we have taken an oath to put the safety of the World first, at all times. My instructions are very clear; I'm to take you straight to the Oracle on a secret Island, only know to us, the Earth Guardians".

Ibi asks, "Who is this Oracle? Is he going to perform some kind of ritual that will give us super skills or powers to do whatever we may have to do?"

Makato contemplates for a moment then answers, "I'm not supposed to tell you much until we get there but actually, we really don't have that much time. The Oracle is a she; she's the priestess of the Egbesu shrine. My duty is to take you to her through Ogoniland to the Island of Bonny".

Ibi is immediately thrown into a sad mood, with tears rolling down her face. Seeing that Ibi is upset, Makato apologises, wondering if he said something to upset Ibi, but the tough lady pulls herself together and tells their host, "I was born in Ogoni. My mother was a princess of Ogoniland, she died giving birth to me…I was told".

The Journey begins

Makato drives through the busy city streets to the country road. He informs his guests that it's a two hour drive to the bank of the Bonny River, an arm of the Niger River delta, from where they will have to take his company speed boat across huge rough waters to the coastal traditional town of Bonny on the large Bonny Island, which lies on the Bight of Bonny; a bay of the Atlantic Ocean.

Makato suggests that the tired travelers take a nap since they'll be having a busy day ahead.

After an hour's drive on the smooth country road, the young heroes wake up.

The stern host hands a food basket over to Ibi.

Ade snatches the food basket from Ibi as he enquires, "You mean you had this full basket of delicious looking snacks all this while?"

Alex struggles to grab the basket from Ade; yelling, "Let me have that!"

Makato is shocked at both guys' ungentlemanly behavior; scolding them, "Where are your manners?"

Both men apologise and ask Ibi, "What will you have, spiced chicken drumstick with fries or the double beef burger?"

They hand over the entire basket to the lady.

Makato continues his drive along the wavy road while the others pass the food basket back and forth amongst one another. Finally Alex lets out a loud burp, making Ade yell, "That's disgusting"; but Ade himself lets out his own violent belch. Everyone in the car finds it funny and the laughter continues as they drive through the winding road.

Alex spoils the fun as he reminds the bunch of the dangerous task they're about to embark upon, "You all do remember that we are about to face a prehistoric celestial super demon and stop him from inviting his friends to take over the World!"

Ibi stresses, "You forgot to add that we could die in the process".

Ade is not ready to stop his unusual good time, replying, "Well, if we are going to die on this mission, we might as well enjoy some great time first".

He calls to their driver from the back seat, "Hey man, can you please play us some cool jams? Give us some real Afro beat".

The straight faced guide smiles and plays a popular Fela Kuti's heavy percussion rhythmic groove.

The four merry travelers mimic the vocals of the music and sway to the beat of the drums. The merriment is sustained as the car zooms along.

They drive to the edge of a beach and they walk through the sand to a pier where Makato's boat is docked.

As they step into the rocking boat, the reality of their perilous mission begins to hit the untested heroes.

Crossing a Threshold

Makato drives the speed boat from the dock, navigating it through the treacherous waters. It doesn't take long before Ade and Alex begin to feel sea sick.

Meanwhile the natural born daughter of the Ijaw Kingdom, masters of the sea; stands confidently at the back of the boat, not holding on to any support; lost in her own thoughts, gazing into the deep blue sea, as if the sea is speaking to her.

Ade asks Makato how he has come to be involved in all this paranormal chase and demon wars.

The straight faced gentleman narrates, "It is a very long story. It all started when my parents immigrated here after my dad was offered a job here to help with the site investigation and soil analysis before the massive construction works of building a floating road network and suspension bridges could commence. Everything went well for a while and my dad soon fell in love with the native people and the land. My mother established a training facility for hydroponic farming as well as a nonprofit veterinary clinic where the villagers came to treat their farm animals. It was all good for the first three years, and then I was born. My father named me Makato, meaning Truth. My dad was a man of honour who believed that a person without integrity is a person who has lost his soul. He used to say, the truth will set you free".

Alex interjects, "Vēritās līberābit vōs; the truth will set you free. It's a verse from the Bible. In John 8, verse 32, Jesus said it while addressing a group of Jews who believed in him".

Makato continues, "My dad was no church goer but he was a very spiritual man. He believed that the World is in us, as we are in the World. He used to say that there are many mysteries in the World, but life itself is not a mystery; you live and you die, simple. It is the lack of understanding of the origin of man and World we occupy that has created the mysteries in life and death".

Alex interjects again, "Vēritās līberābit vōs.

He tells their host, "It sounds so simple, yet still complex to imagine and you are beginning to sound like the wise old Seer at the Monastery".

Makato nods and replies, "I trained under him for a time. After my parents died, he came and took me with him. I lived with him; even through my education, until I became an adult and got this job".

Makato pauses, trying to fight back his emotions, then continues, "Anyway, everything changed one rainy day; I was five years old and like all children, I was alone playing with my paper boat near the river when something dragged me into the river.

I can't remember how I got out but when I did, I was told that I was gone for several days, even though to me, it felt just like a few minutes. I couldn't find my parents anywhere.

The villagers told me that my parents both dived into the river after me, trying to rescue me, but they too became lost. The villagers said they must have drowned but their bodies where never found. After many years of living with the Seer, I learned that there are things we know and there are many that we don't; we must learn to accept it and move on. What matters is for each and every one of us to find our purpose in this life and fulfill it and hopefully, the World can become a much better place. So, everyday, I remember what my father taught me; that is to live a modest life and keep for yourself only what you need to survive; amassing wealth to be at the top will only make you feel lonely. He used to say that the loneliest place in the World is at the top; the higher you go, the lonelier you become".

Smiling to himself, the well-built guide concludes, "His favourite saying was; when someone has stopped glowing, he'll seek the spotlight, yet the one who glows from within, takes the attention. Let your peace, joy and wealth come from within. Your generosity is your peace, your love is your joy, and your talent is your wealth. These are given to you to light-up the world".

Welcome to Ogoni

Makato navigates the boat through the brackish mangrove waters of the Island, to the long stretch of the welcoming beach of the Finima Town. They get off the boat without wasting any time and move straight to the village of Akiama. The village is a small trading settlement with well-planned narrow streets and modern built houses. As they walk through the town, weary residents come out to catch a glimpse of the strangers. Makato, being familiar with the Island takes the three companions to the house of the village head; Chief Ebi Kabaka; who welcomes the visitors with Kola nuts; the West African symbol of hospitality, friendship and respect.

Makato wastes no time, he tells Chief Kabaka that they are there to see the Priestess. The village head replies in the affirmative, "Yes, the Oracle has sent word to me already; we have been waiting for you. You will be most welcome to stay in my house; but first you must eat, you have travelled from far".

The Chief leads them to the inner court where they are served, a delicious meal of Kekefiyai; a pottage made with chopped unripen plantain, fish, other sea food and palm oil.

As they eat, Chief Kabaka tells the guests about the enemy and the impossible task ahead. He tells them that his people have long dreaded and expected this day, but look forward to eliminating the dark shadow that has long spread its evil tentacles over the entire region and the World.

He adds, "People have been disappearing in many villages in Ogoniland, across the Bonny River, they believe a terrible evil exist there".

After the meal, the host shows his visitors their sleeping quarters and informs them that he will take them to see the Oracle in the morning.

As he leaves his guest to rest, he adds, "The Oracle is a hundred years old, she is very wise; she alone knows what we must do. She is the keeper of the shrine of Egbesu, the god of warfare of we the Ijaw people. Its force can only be used in defense or to correct an injustice, and only by people who are in harmony with the Universe; the mark of his divine force is Ẹdụlẹ́, the Panther. Rest well now and may your dreams be pleasant".

Meeting the Oracle

The next morning, Makato takes his leave, he tell his three companions that he must go back to the mainland but will be back in three days and meet them at the shrine of the ancient warrior and deity. Chief Kabaka then leads the other young visitors through the winding barely visible pathway of the bordering jungle to the forbidden Monkey Forest. As they make their way through the dark forest, a large number of feral Mandrills trail the trespassers. The primates are barely seen as they hide behind the thick mangrove forest. The wild protectors of the forest maintain their distance but join in the trail through the misty forest. After about an hour of following the humans, the primates suddenly disappear and soon after Chief Kabaka leads his company out from the dark forest into a beautiful garden; the home of the keepers of the Egbesu shrine.

The village chief stops his team and makes the call to announce the arrival of the visitors to the sacred garden. Soon after, a line of well adorned maidens appears from within the depth of the garden; and walking closely behind them is the revered Oracle.

The Priestess greets the visitors and walks straight up to Ibi, calling her by her full name, "Ibinabo, Bearer of Good Tidings, you have your mother's eyes".

Ibi eagerly asks, "You knew my mother?"

The Priestess nods as she touches Ibi's necklace, answering, "She was my pupil; the strongest".

As if ignoring the other members of Ibi's group, the Oracle recalls her memory of Ibi's mother, "Your mother met a man, a foreigner, who worked for the oil company; they were very much in love; not long after they were married and then they moved to back to her village in Kibani, across the river. They suffered many trials; not from people, but from the dark shadows. Your mother was tormented constantly in her dreams by the evil one, which sort to drive her crazy but your mother was a strong willed woman, who had the heart of a hunter; we called her Ẹdụlẹ́, the Panther".

Still speaking directly to Ibi, the old woman continued, "Your parents stood their ground; holding on strong, believing that their love would endure; but their love was not enough to save her. When she was pregnant with a child, your mother knew what she must do to save her unborn child and fulfill the Prophesy which foretold that her seed would destroy the evil one".

Then side stepping to Ade, the Oracle calls out, "Adebowale, descendant of the great line of Kings, I see you have struggled to embrace who you are and so you are not ready to accept the task that is appointed to you". Ade looks away from the Priestess as he tries to hide his rage but the wise old woman catches Ade's expression. She gently places her left hand on the side of Ade's face and brings his gaze directly into hers.

She admonishes Ade in a stern voice, "Your anger is fed by revenge; be careful, many who sort vengeance most times end up with regret. If you must be angry, let it be against the one evil which has set brother against brother and nations against nations; in whose plans there is never a victor, instead all sides are vanquished. Your youthful fury is your strength but your impatience will rob you and even the World of victory over the one enemy whose singular mission is to destroy the World of men; therefore I encourage you to put your past behind you and embrace your call to serve, knowing that you stand for many and in good company; together with whom you will triumph and bring an end to the darkness which has cast a shadow over all mankind since the beginning of man's existence".

A sudden calmness seem to envelope Ade after the profound words of the Oracle. Ade remains quiet as he reflects on the importance of the clarion call.

The three companions bow in reverence as the priestess takes a few steps backwards to assess the readiness of the young heroes; then addressing the group she warned, "None of you have chosen yourself but each one of you must decide on your own whether or not you will honour the call".

Then walking close to Alex, her face almost touching his, she whispers to him, "Alexander, your name means the people's defender; give me your hands".

Alex is reluctant; instead he turns to Ibi as if to ask for her approval. Ibi frowns at his rude hesitation so Alex stretches both hands towards the old woman. The priestess gently takes Alex's hands and smiles as she reads his palms, "Your unwillingness is fueled by self-doubt; a good trait which brings caution to one's action, but remember, one cannot get to one's destination standing fixed at a point. It is in facing challenges that we find our courage".

She lets go of the young man's hands and places both of her hands on Alex's bowed head and speaks more firmly, "You have the gift of the Inner Eye, yet you do not see. You must trust in the goodness of your heart to guide your decisions and you must take a chance on your loved ones; if you don't you will lose something precious but if you do, your Eye of Consciousness will become open and you will begin to see what others cannot perceive".

The Oracle then walks up to the chief and asks, "Where is he?"

In a humble pose, Chief Kabaka answers, "Makato has gone ahead to prepare, he shall meet us in three days' time".

The Priestess turns away and smiles then replies, "Good, he already knows what he must do. He has a lot at stake and much to fight for. The spirits of his parents are still enslaved by that vile demon; the Prince of the deep; who took them when they fought the evil creature in the depths of the river as they tried to save their little child, thirty years ago. That demon has since returned from whence it came, halfway around the World from the great sea of the East".

The Oracle then takes Ibi's hand and leads her alone into a distant hut where they both stayed for a long time.

She tells Ibi that the enemy vowed to pollute the entire race of man, thereby making foul, the most treasured creation of God. Over time, the servants of the dark side crept into the lives of men, offering them the pleasures that men desired, but in the end, he claims the precious fire burning in them, laying waste generations upon generations of man.

For an empty man will always seek to fill the void in him, craving more and more of things that will always return to dust. Man's desires has become endless and his greed   insatiable; thereby becoming such a being that is more of dust and less divine. So, the enemy's plan is almost complete as the children of God have forgotten who they are and have become corrupted. Now that all is as it was planned, and the peoples of the World have turned completely away from the light and have embraced pleasure and false freedom that is promised, darkness and a new World will be unveiled and the five commanders of hell on Earth will begin to merge both Worlds, creating a new World of damnation.

When she returns with Ibi, she tell them of the many battles that have been fought but were continually lost because the race of men have not unified as one, but now for the first time, pure blood children of man will join forces with descendants of the original guardians bringing hope which has faded over time. She however warned that weapons of mortal men will not destroy these supernatural beings that have existed before mankind itself. The four chosen ones, Ade, Ibinabo, Alex and Makato must separately journey through the four passages of space and time to retrieve the sacred weapons of the ancient celestial guardians.

She also cautions the new heroes, saying, "Some have passed through the gates but never returned".

Looking worried herself, the Oracle continued, "I cannot tell you what you will encounter beyond the gates; it is for you to discover yourselves. If all four of you do not succeed, then the fate of the entire human race will be doomed".

She then instructs Chief Kabaka, "It is time to wake up the warrior god. It is not something that has been done before, I know it's dangerous but we need all the help we can get. I will offer the necessary sacrifice. The wrath of the god of war cannot be contained by mere mortals so we need to wait for Ṣàngó to recover his full strength and come to the shrine as well. Then and only then can we dare to awake a god that has slept for many generations".

She sends the visitors away with their host and commands him to bring the young heroes to the sacred shrine of Egbesu three days later.

CHAPTER 7: WAITING FOR ŞÀNGÓ

An Ancestry Revealed

Back at the village of Akiama, the three companions pondering over what the Oracle revealed to them, they decide to explore the meandering walkways of the peaceful village. Alex asks Ibi, "You were gone for a long time with the Oracle, what did she say to you?"

Ibi stares ahead, as if to relive the tale she just heard. After a moment of silence, Ibi begins to narrate what the old woman told her, "She took me into a hut and ordered the maidens to stay outside; I had a feeling immediately that what she was going to tell me would not be pleasant. Staring at my pendant, she held it in both of her hands and with a sad expression, she turned toward me and asked me to sit down. We both sat on a bamboo bench and she said to me; *The Unborn Child has returned*. I did not understand but I didn't say anything because I expected that there was more to follow. She told me that my pendant belonged to my mother; I interrupted her and asked if she knew my mother. She nodded her head and answered; *she died while giving birth to you.*

I told her that I knew that already, my dad told me all about it and that was why he had to take me with him back to England.

The Priestess continued, *Hmm! That's not all. Your mother knew that her life and that of her unborn child was in danger. There was a Prophesy; it was said that a woman born of the royal family of Kibani in Ogoniland will be the vanquisher of the evil whose shadow had cast a tremendous fear in our land for many generations. From the time of your great-grandmother, we have watched out for signs when the chosen one will be born but we did not get the revelation from our ancestors. When your mother was born, we knew without a doubt that she was the one. However, we didn't realise then that what was revealed to us was that she would carry the seed. For the bearer of the seed was as important as the seed itself. All through her pregnancy, your mother was tormented both in her dreams and in her awaken life. We fortified her with charms and markings to protect her from the powerful evil. While we all were afraid of what may happen to her and fate of our land and indeed all mankind if the dark one gets to her, your mother was not afraid, in her state of pregnancy, she believed that light would always triumph over darkness.*

Your father was often away at work, sometimes for days, but he didn't fully appreciate our ways and the power of the evil we faced. However, he knew that we were all worried and most times scared for the safety of his wife, so he did what any man would do to protect his family. One morning, without our knowledge, he took your mother away from Kibani to the city of Port-Harcourt, where he believed your mother would get proper medical care. I sent several messengers to him but he said his wife was being properly looked after in the well-equipped hospital run by the oil company where he worked. One night close to her delivery date, your mother went into a coma. While in the coma, she was murmuring words the hospital did not understand; they were even more puzzled that someone in a coma could speak, nonstop. This continued for two nights but the doctors assured your father that she was probably agitated because of her high fever and that her utterances where only symptoms of an involuntary nervous phenomenon. One night she suddenly opened her eyes, screaming and calling for your father to bring her back to this village. The hospital tried to restrain her but your father agreed to her wishes. He brought your mother back to their home and he sent for me..."

...When the time came for you to be born, your mother knew what she must do to save her unborn child...

...Though your father did not understand, your mother insisted that I prepare her for the ultimate warrior battle. We performed the sacred ritual and in spirit she became a true Ẹdụlẹ́, the hunter Panther. Though her body was weak, her spirit was very strong and ready to fight for the protection of her unborn child. Your mother knew that the battle would claim her life and like all mother Panthers, she was ready to fight to the death to protect her child. She made me promise that I would deliver you from her lifeless body if the battle is lost. Your father stayed by her side, assuring her that all would be well, but he could not hold back his tears as he could not help his beloved wife in anyway at her vulnerable time. Your mother kissed her husband and smiled, telling him that there was no other way...

...She made him promise to do whatever it will take to protect you and raise you as a true daughter of the Ogoni people. She looked at me and with a bold expression, she said to me; I will hold them back; and with those words, she took her last breath. I fulfilled my promise and brought you out from her lifeless body. Your eyes were already open and as you announced your arrival with a shrieking cry, your peering blue eyes peered into mine and I immediately knew that you were the one; the prophesied deliverer of our people. I removed the necklace from your mother's neck and so the family heirloom passed on to you. I wore it around your neck; and I proclaimed your name to the World as Ibinabo, Bearer of good tidings. Your father wept uncontrollably, blaming himself for not taking care of his pregnant wife; he did not understand that there was nothing he could have done to protect his wife and that his destined job was always to protect you and not your mother. While your father mourned the loss of your mother, the village celebrated the bravery of their late Ẹdụlẹ and the birth of a new hunter warrior. The sacred pendant passed on to you, as a symbol of the Sacred Panther and to remind you always of who you are and where you come from".

Ibi continues her sad story as she walks with Ade and Alex, "Ever since I have worn the Pendant, never removing it, because it's the only the thing I have of my mother. The entire experience was too much for my father to handle; he gave up his job here and moved us both to England. He became over-protective of me, not letting me out of his sight, not even for a minute. I was home schooled until I was fifteen".

Ibi carries on with her strange tale, "Ever since we got on that boat from Port-Harcourt, I've had this weird feeling that this place is calling to me. I seem to know my way around here; I don't know but it seems like I have lived here before; how do you explain that?"

Ade puts his arm around Ibi, comforting the obviously distressed girl; as Alex watches the tough guy showing his first emotional side for the first time since they've all known one another.

They stop their walk momentarily as Ibi leans over to Ade and places her head on Ade broad shoulders. Ade hugs Ibi with his right arm and with his left pulls Alex close for a group hug; then they continue their walk.

Recalling a Haunting Memory

The three continue their stroll and Alex asks Ibi, "How come you never had any premonitions about this or even a dream; or is it the place that has steered this feeling you're having?"

Ibi shakes her head as she tries to make sense of it all, "I really don't know myself but who knows, it's probably all the mysteries of the past couple of days or maybe as you said, it's being here, that is steering it up".

Ade cuts in, "It could be all that. When I first met Ṣàngó, he always said that we are all connected somehow and that sometimes, that connection becomes strong when our deepest feelings are set free. So maybe the Oracles revelations opened up your deep feelings and being here makes it easy for you to connect to your mother's memories of this place".

Alex interjects, "Poor you Ibi, I can't even beginning to think how I would feel if someone throws that much revelation unto me".

Ade again reassuring Ibi, he adds, "Look at it from the bright side, at least now you know a lot more about your origin and more importantly, about the bravery and honour of your mother".

Alex too agrees, "Yes, I now know where you got all that confidence and fighting spirit you've exhibited growing up back in London".

Ibi smiles and gives both guys a peck each on their cheeks, thanking them for making her feel much better.

Tapping Ade on his head, Ibi asks boldly, "What about you? You have always kept to yourself; no one knows anything about you, other that the obvious fact that you were adopted by your lovely parents, the Reverends Brown".

Ade hesitates, doubling his pace and walks ahead of his friends. Alex and Ibi catch-up with him and pulling Ade back, Ibi insists, "You are not getting off that easy. Common, we are the heroes of the World, remember; we are a team now and teammates don't stand alone, all for one and one for all, as they say".

The three friends walk up to a wooden bridge and Ade stops, gazing over the gleaming river far into the horizon, he recounts his long repressed past, "I was seven years old when I left my beautiful town".

Looking sad, the strong man of Vintage Street betrays his vulnerability as he continues, "I never wished to leave my rich homeland of Óké-Ífẹ̀ here in Nigeria. The King had just joined the ancestors and my father, coming from one of the ruling houses was favoured to be the new King. Many of the chiefs were afraid that my father might reform the entire Kingdom and maybe change the long established ways of several generation of Kings before him. My father believed that traditions should be dynamic and so should change as the needs of the people changed. He believed that it is the place of Kings to make the sacrifice for his people and not sit on high thrones like mini deities, getting fat with their lazy Princes and spoilt Princesses living ostentatiously while the people go hungry. He also openly condemned corrupt politicians who also connived with these merciless rulers to deprive the masses of their much needed farm lands thereby causing food scarcity and hunger which in turn creates divisions and crises amongst the various ethnic and religious groups. As the poverty, lack and want spreads across the lands, the overfed ruling class impose taxes and other debilitating hardship, leaving majority of the people without much hope.

My father never hesitated to state his displeasure and often walked out of many council meetings, knowing fully well that the rulers were set in their ways. Not long he began to observe that strange and threatening things started happening around our house; unexplained fires suddenly ravaged our farms and properties. My mother feared for my father's life as well as hers and mine, their only child. She pleaded with my father to stay clear of the elders and council members, knowing fully well that those people will stop at nothing to get rid of anyone who dares get in their way. One afternoon, after the completion of the burial rites of the late King, my father was called to the palace for an urgent meeting by the king makers, possibly to decide on who the mantle of kingship would fall. His most trusted friend, Chief Adeoye, the Baálę; something like the Mayor; of our village cautioned my father and tried to stop him from attending the suspicious meeting but my father insisted he would answer the call of the council, assuring us that Olódùmarè, the Supreme God would protect him. That was the last we saw of my father. News came to us later that evening that my father had choked while dining with the elders after the meeting but we believe he was poisoned. We were not allowed to see his body for fear that the cause of his death may be discovered; we were told that it was traditional for the Chief Priest to cleanse the body of any evil spirits else a bad omen would plague the town. That night, several armed guards invaded our home looking for me. That night Chief Adeoye took me into the nearby forest and stayed with me all night. In the morning, my mother said the guards promise to come back and if she did not surrender me, they would lock her in the dungeon, where she would be tortured and treated like a traitor. She packed some bread and water in a sack and rubbed coconut oil all over my body and hid me in the deep well in our compound. The oil would protect me from mosquito and other insect bites and also mask my scent, when the guards come searching. She lowered me into the deep dark well with the draw-rope and covered the top with dried palm-fronds leaves.

That morning, the enraged guards charged into our compound rampaging through the many huts and tearing down every door in the house. Not getting what they came for, they dragged my mother outside and beat her with sticks as they yelled at her, threatening her to hand me over to them. Hearing her screaming and wailing, I wanted to come out of hiding and defend my mother from the bullies but I knew that a little seven year-old, like myself wouldn't stand a chance and my mother may be in greater danger if she tries to stop them from taking me away. Believing that I had run away from the town, they left. I stayed in well for three days, enduring the nonstop buzzing high pitch noise of hundreds of mosquitoes in my ears and the formication of crawling cockroaches on my skin. My mother brought me out of the well on the third day and wrapped me in an old cloth and tied pieces of broken barrel wood around me. She carried me on her head, pretending to be carrying firewood to the market for sale. She walked through the town with the load on her head, without   anyone suspecting anything. Outside the town she untied the bunch and we both walked for hours to a distant village where we saw a small church building. Hungry and exhausted, my mother and I fell asleep on the floor.

It was at that moment a missionary couple, the Reverends Mr. and Mrs. Brown found us and took us to their home. The nice couple tended to my mother's wounds and scratches on my body. They also gave us food and offered us shelter. My mother pleaded with the Missionaries to take care of me because she insisted that she must go back to our town to bury her husband. I clasped on to her, begging her not to go back; we both cried as she pulled away. She made me promise to survive wherever I found myself and have a good life. I lived with Browns in the town for a few years, spending most of my time roaming the streets with street urchins and learning the ropes, as they say. When the Reverends work was done in the town, they moved to East Africa and took me with them. I traveled with them to many counties as they continued their missionary work. I never saw my mother again and the childless Browns adopted me, so I became their only child, attending good schools and getting the best parental love any child could wish for. A year ago, my new parents retired from active missionary life and returned to their home Country, England. That was how I came to live on Vintage Street".

A Son's Regret

After Ade's poignant tale, Ibi cuddles the stoic guy in a tight embrace. Also stunned by the intense story, Alex commends Ade saying, "I can't even begin to process what I would do in that situation".

Looking flabbergasted he continues, "I mean, hearing one's mom's screams as she's being attacked by wild men and not being able to do anything about it".

Looking sad, he turns to Ade and Ibi and laments, "Both of you have experienced unimaginable traumatic events. My life has always been ordinary; well, apart from the fact that my mom walked out on us. I guess she was fed-up of my dad's constant drift into his own World, consumed by his conspiracy theories, especially the end of the World invasion theory. He even went on so much about how he believes that some organisations meet regularly and how they might be controlling many aspects of our everyday living. I didn't believe him; I mean, no one did, we thought he was a nutcase. Every year he would go to these science conventions where he presents his absurd imaginary parabolic map within Africa; claiming that there is a rift or interdimensional portal through which superior extraterrestrial beings could invade our World.

While he was going all around making a fool of himself, our financial situation at home wasn't what you'll call stable. He was barely holding on to his job; his company only kept him because his fantasies created a continuous satire which was featured regularly in the company's commercial magazine and that brought in substantial revenue from the young generation, who for whatever reasons lapped his crazy theories. My mom and I had to take menial jobs to support in paying our accumulating bills".

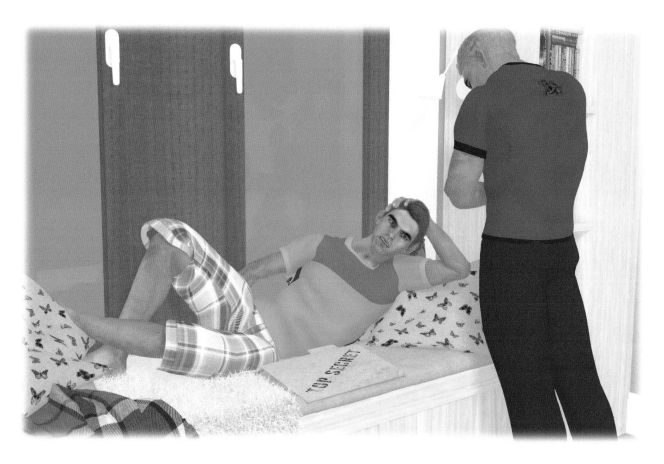

Ibi disagrees with Alex; saying, "I don't think you're giving your dad due credit here; after all, he is the only one in the science community who has discovered the Earth invasion phenomenon that we ourselves are just coming to terms with".

Ade nods in agreement. Alex sighs and with a penitence face, he recalls, "Yes, you're both right, but despite all what we have heard and the strange things that have happened to us in the last couple of days, the whole thing still sounds incredible. However, looking back at how I treated him, I kind of feel that I betrayed him. Family should stand with one another, no matter what; I mean, even if I didn't believe him, I should at least have supported him".

Alex begins to cry as he repeats to himself, "I betrayed him…I betrayed him!"

Ibi puts her arm around Alex and offers comforting words, "Things that happen to you don't define you; so don't become that. You should define yourself by what you believe and the things that you can do. It doesn't matter what anyone thinks or says about you. People can be inconsistent, saying something nice today then nasty next time. We must develop the ability that is latent in us and grab the opportunities which come our way. Your Talent is your ability and every event in your life opens up a new opportunity".

As the mood becomes surreal, the three friends contemplate in their own thoughts as they each stand on the bridge staring into the horizon.

The Village Party

Later that night, their host, Chief Kabaka, invites his three guests to the *Feast of Bloom*, the one night every year when young men and women over the age of eighteen mingle freely under a bright Moonlight and the night is climaxed with the annual maiden prerogative dance; when a girl is free to choose any guy she has secretly admired.

At midnight, Ibi walks to the party ground flanked on either side by Ade and Alex. The trio are dressed in native hand-woven colourful body-hugging attire; Ibi's showing her entire legs up to her upper thigh while Ade's and Alex's clothing are just tight colourful shorts wrapped with dyed raffia leaves, without any shirts, their generously oiled bodies shine in the bright moonlight. The three friends are excited and for the first time, they truly seem to be relaxed as they wobble through the dense beach sand that lead them to a wide grass clearing which is well delineated by a circle of flaming torches. Inside the circle are long bamboo benches buried firmly in the ground near each warm flaming torch.

Leisurely, several hefty male drummers file out and take up seating positions as if already allotted.

The drumming begins and soon their rhythmic music welcomes another row of elaborately adorned young girls who dance and wriggle their waists sensually, deliberately to attract the already mesmerized males.

Dozens of beautiful maidens take their seats, while still swaying to the beat of the drums.

Soon a seemingly unending row of warrior-like young men dressed in white shorts with wrap-around skirts made from the same dyed raffia leaves like those of Ade and Alex; march into the circle, stumping the ground and causing the bamboo seats to vibrate, creating their own clacking sounds. There are no elders around, only young men and women, aged between eighteen and twenty-one.

Tonight, like all nights of the *Feast of Bloom,* many couples may be paired for life. It is a woman's night when the ladies have the right to choose whomever they desire. The men, on the other hand must accept being chosen otherwise he will be fined a healthy live goat for every proposal he refuses. The night is an age-long tradition of which a couple can be betrothed at first sight. It was created to give women the unique opportunity to choose freely the man she likes. To give the girls a show of the men's character and strength, the young men must each pick an opponent and wrestle until one opponent surrenders or one is declared defeated by the umpire. Not participating in the wrestling bout reduces a guy's chances of being chosen by a maiden.

After the wrestling session all males must participate in a series of exhausting dance routines. The men are then allowed to rest while the maidens serve them with freshly tapped Palm wine; this is when the maidens try to entice the men by showing how well they'll care for their future husbands and this is also the time for the maidens to flaunt their beauty.

Alex and Ade cunningly evade both the wrestling and complicated warrior dance sessions but eagerly partake in the Palm wine refreshments. After performing the formal rituals of the night, the drummers play more music while the men and women mingle. A long table of steaming hot Seafood, various mixed fruit juices and Palm wine is laid out for everyone to serve themselves.

Ade and Alex get intoxicated by the sweet Palm wine and soon begin to chase each other around the field, but their childish games are soon interrupted when Ade is dragged into the circle by a tall beautiful girl who seems to be the girl all the boys have their eyes on, Ibi looks on as another girl yanks Alex to the dance circle and he is soon dropped and picked again by a plus size girl with a large hip, who seems to want Alex for keeps. The couples matching dance continues with every girl picking a guy and drag him to the center of the dance circle and then dumping him and going back to pick another, as if she is having a tasting session. This process goes on until the entire atmosphere is turned into a chaotic frenzy of dancing and merriment.

Ibi seems to be isolated and so dances alone all through the night until she gets a tap on the shoulder; it's Ade, they both dance the couples matching dance; while Alex romps on the soft grass under a pile of giggling girls.

Ade and Ibi kiss and hold hands as they walk away from the loud noise of the party to a cluster of Coconut trees, where they lay on a soft purple bed of flowering Zebrina ground covers. They remain in a prolong cuddle as if they have waited for this moment all their lives.

Far from the madding crowd, Ade and Ibi could hear Alex's high pitch laughter being drowned by the loud drumming. Ibi cocoons herself in Ade's strong arms and tells her chosen man, "I wish this night will go on forever".

Ade kisses the pretty girl on her forehead and looks a bit sad as he replies his new found love, "You know, they say time flies when you're having fun. I now know what they mean because it seems the night is running too fast and there is no way for me to stop it".

Together they respond simultaneously, "Let's just enjoy it while it lasts".

CHAPTER 8: THE GOD OF WAR

Welcome the Samurai

On the morning of the third day, Ade and Ibi are up early, not because it is the appointed day which the Oracle has requested that Chief Kabaka and the three young heroes must gather and be prepared for the waking of the war deity, Egbesu but because the two newly matched couple can't wait to be together after the excitement of the previous night's romantic bond. The two love-birds seat on a wooden bench in the village garden; both lost in the euphoria of their newly found love. Soon they are joined by Alex, who is just waking up from his Palm wine induced hangover. Ade teases the still moaning pal, "How's your fiancée, or should I say fiancées?"

Alex replies sarcastically, "I thought we three are heroes-in-crime? You vanished and left me alone to deal with scary combination of sweet booze and richly endowed damsels".

Ibi joins Ade to tease their whimpering mate, "You mean plus-sized ladies".

Ade and Ibi still entangled in their romantic cuddle, laugh as Alex desperately tries to shake himself to full sobriety .

The comical scene of the three friends is disrupted by the sudden emergence of Makato. Dressed in full Samurai garb with a real Katana packed behind in a scabbard. Makato steps boldly towards the startled trio. Alex challenges the battle ready buddy, asking the straight-faced Ninja looking pal, "Where have you been man, and what's with the Ninja clothes?"

Makato removes the sword and sheath from his back and squeezes himself besides Ade on the wooden bench. He wastes no time to relieve his companions from their shock by going straight to narrating what he has been up to, "I travelled back to my home, the ancient town of Aizu-Wakamatsu in Japan. What I'm wearing belonged to my grandfather, Kiyoshi Kishimoto; the last warrior of the Saigo no Otoko clan; my clan.

My family was tasked with the sacred responsibility to stop the invasion of evil spirits and demons. They were called the Saigo, meaning last defense. My grandfather tried to pass on this honourable responsibility to my father but my father refused to accept his call. My father saw his own grandfather and father killed fighting powerful forces of darkness. He argued that men were not supposed to do the work of the gods and no man can stop such strong adversaries who have existed for many centuries; even before time itself. He decided to leave my home town and Japan completely, travelling far away to a place where he would be safe and live a normal life, so he took up a job with a geo-seismic company and volunteered to be posted here in Port-Harcourt, Nigeria where he can make meaningful contributions to the lives of others.

It was here that he met my mother, who was a veterinary doctor, working with a local government agency, providing the needed veterinary services to native farmers with their livestock and teaching young women to raise high protein crustaceans, here in Ogoni. They had a happy life here and everything went well and I was born. My father was happy and even forgot about the lives and role of his forefathers. A few years after I was born, my parents began to experience visions of an impending attack by the dreaded water demon, Dagon".

Alex mutters, "Not that Dagon, the fish god, half-man, half-fish creature?"

Makato nods and continues his mystical tale, "Yes, that Dagon, only he is not just a fishlike creature, he takes many forms, and the sea is his domain. He was the evil one that took me as a child and kept me captive beneath the depths of the sea. I did not know it then, but I was under the sea for several days, though down under it seemed like only a few minutes. It was while I was imprisoned by Dagon that my parents dived into the sea, down to the abyss where the creature ruled. During the battle with the creature, my parents set me free but paid the supreme price themselves. I was taken to the Oracle, and it was the old Priestess who broke the spell that I was under and the memory of the lost three days under water was unlocked. I then remembered how my father evoked the supernatural power of the Saigo No Otoko and fought the water demon and his many sea devils. My mother brought me to the surface and to the shore but she went back into the sea because my father was outnumbered. Sadly both of them never resurfaced. Some local fishermen found me on the far side of the island and brought me back to the Priestess. For many years as I grew-up, I had the same nightmare of my parents surrounded and trapped under the sea. Thanks to the Priestess, I was delivered from the nightmares but she told me that my parents' souls were still trapped in the realm of Dagon and the only way they can be set free is for Dagon himself to be destroyed. Now, I come prepared to do battle with Dagon and his fellow demons who think they can take our World from us. My father thought he could run away from his destiny and live a normal life, but as you now know, that the life he so much sought after still eluded him. It seems one cannot run away from one's fate and that is why I have to face mine".

The four companions pause for a while then Makato tells his companions that it time to meet the Oracle.

Waking a Sleeping Giant

Makato leads his three companions to the Oracle who is already waiting for them. She dips a bunch of fresh leaves in a white clay pot containing a portion and sprinkles the blessed water on the four chosen ones, reciting inaudible incantations as she showers the group. The Priestess leads the company along a trail through the forest. As they walk to the edge of the forest Ade reminds the Oracle, "Ṣàngó is not here".

Makato responds, "We can no longer wait for him, we do not have much time, it has to be done now".

The priestess momentarily hesitates but agrees with Makato that they have run out of time, "You're right, we can no longer delay". The old woman then assures the group, beckoning to them in her usual squeaky voice, "He will be here; come, let us begin".

As the group emerge from the forest, Chief Kabaka is seen far ahead beating several huge Dumdum drums; he is a lone drummer creating the complex drumbeats which fills the air, transforming the hither to serene environment of the Egbesu shrine, which has laid quiet for ages to a raucous reverberating ambience.

The Chief seems to be in trance as he ignores the advancing company. He drums away, dancing and yelling in a frenzy.

The Oracle moves to the side and begins to recite some kind of ancient incantations. Sparks of electricity starts to appear in front of her. The streaks of lightning grow wildly and jump to a huge rock-head statue buried into the ground at the shrine. As the drumming and the incantations become more intense, the rock statue begins to vibrate vigorously. Ibi and her two pals step backwards but the captivated Japanese Samurai warrior stands confidently and eagerly awaiting for whatever will materialise from the statue.

As the environment becomes intensely energized, the rock head begins to crack. Seeing the unfolding phenomenon, the young heroes step further away from the vibrating huge rock-head. Suddenly, there is a blast and the huge rock-head is shattered into several large pieces; each piece is flung in a different direction, knocking the dancing Chief and his drums over. The explosion is followed by a deafening roar and a raging giant man emerges from the clearing smoke. Flashes of electricity clings to the towering giant who looks both angry and surprised at the little people who surround him. The raging giant pulls out a huge sword from his back scabbard, ready to strike his perceived enemies, just then another loud roar is heard from behind, followed by pounding steps.

Ṣàngó arrives just in time to accost the fierce giant.

The awoken giant confronts the intruders, "Who dares disturb the rest of Egbesu?"

The Priestess kneels and recites a continuous poetry of praises, honouring the furious deity.

Ṣàngó yells out as he stomps into the shattered shrine, "Egbesu, the Lord of wars! Do you want to sleep forever?"

Ṣàngó laughs out loud as he comes face to face with his equally sized giant.

Egbesu queries the approaching fiery mate, "You?"

Ṣàngó replies the angry waking friend in his trademark booming voice, "Welcome back, my brother; it seems you have been disturbed from the pleasures of a blissful dream".

Egbesu is not amused by Ṣàngó's flattery; looking around at the frightened humans; the towering giant asks, "Are these little ones with you?"

Makato gazes at the sword-wielding giant in awe as he recognises the ancient sword of a legendary black warrior; he pays his respects to the deity with a deep long bow as he yells in supplication, "Yasuke!"

The Priestess, still kneeling, continues her éloges, "Oh great god of warfare, defender of the Izon kingdom, the mighty warrior and justice dispenser. We humbly call upon you at our great time of need, for darkness seeks to extinguish the light in our World".

Şàngó's light mood changes suddenly to a stern expression as he discloses the unpleasant news to the war god, "They are back and this time all hell is being emptied upon us".

Egbesu, pointing his huge sword towards Ṣàngó's smaller companions, he enquires, "Who are your friends and why do they bow before me?"

Ṣàngó answers, "These are the brave young heroes of men who have joined with us to do battle against the enemy".

Egbesu, still puzzled, asks vehemently, "But why do they keep bowing before me?"

Ṣàngó smiles as he replies his new mate, "They think we are gods".

Both giants burst into a fit of laughter. Egbesu questions further, "Why will they think that when they are the pure born children of the Creator of all things".

Ṣàngó shakes his head as he also is puzzled, saying, "Well, tell them yourself, maybe they will listen to you".

Egbesu gets back to Ṣàngó's initial unsettling revelation, as if he is asking for confirmation, "What do you mean, who is back?"

The Priestess gets up from her kneeling posture and confirms the troubling matter, "Yes, great one. The Prince of darkness is planning a comeback. His strongest and most vile servants have ruled over and corrupted many areas of human life. In a few days they plan to open a gateway between their foul realm and our World here in Ogoni. We are outnumbered and in fact not with much hope; but these young heroes, chosen by the gods have come to join forces with us. We here, my lord, are all that stand between the forces of darkness and the future of mankind and maybe with our combined strength and knowledge, we can stand a chance against our great enemy".

The towering giants ponder for a moment then Makato steps forward bravely to address the demigods, "I am Makato, son of Kishimoto, descendant of the Clan of Saigo No Otoko; The last Defense. For many generations my family has kept watch and defended the World against many invasions of demons from land, sea and sky. I do not fear them and with your supreme powers, I believe we shall triumph".

A Declaration of War

Ṣàngó acknowledges the brave Samurai, "Yes Makato, son of Kishimoto, descendant of the noble Saigo No Otoko clan. It is true that your family has fought many battles against the forces of darkness and has been victorious. However, this is not just a battle; it is the ultimate war, the Armageddon, the end of days. Hell is going to unleash its most powerful and ruthless demons. They are not like the marauding imps you have heard of. These are generals of hell itself, they are the ancient angels who united with the Prince of darkness himself to wage the unholy war against the angels of the most high; they are the fallen angels of old. They were part the builders of the foundations of this World, they have watched it grow and even now many traitors of men have joined forces with the dark side to destroy the World and make it an extension of hell. Egbesu and I have fought one of them before; Brutus Demonicus the dreaded one; whose real name is Belial. He is the leader of the dark World on Earth. The combined might of Egbesu and I was no match for Brutus and his legion".

The Priestess exclaims, "And that is where our young heroes come in. Each of them must pass through a separate Gate of Virtue and retrieve the lost weapons of the ancient Watchers".

Egbesu is hesitant, reminding the Oracle, "Many have tried but failed and did not return, dead or trapped, we do not know. These are gates of Virtue, only the pure at heart stand a chance. Each time a Seeker fails to retrieve a weapon, that gate collapses forever. There are only four gates left, we cannot afford to lose any of the last four celestial weapons; we have to be sure they will succeed".

After the Oracle and Sàngó narrate the near impossible perilous quest, Egbesu tells Sàngó, if all you are saying is true then it is futile trying to face the might of adversary without seeking more help. The Oracle answers the war god saying, "We have no one else, you here are all that the World has to stop this great evil". Egbesu then cynically calls to Sàngó, "Then you must call out to your brother".

Sàngó furiously replies the teasing giant, "He is not my brother and I will not fight by his side. He is my …"

Before Sàngó can finish his sentence, Egbesu interrupts him saying, "He is not your enemy, in fact both of you are like twins, you wield similar arms and both of you command the forces of lightning and thunder". Then with a smirk on his face Egbesu teases the already furious Thunder deity, "Except that he is more good looking; at least she seemed to think so".

Sàngó snaps into a mild frenzy as he disagrees with Egbesu's insinuations, "She was never attracted to that clown of a deity. Bilikisu was the embodiment of beauty, a glowing petal floating in a sea all by herself; she was mine, at least before the clown confused her".

Egbesu laughs out loudly as he points to the resentful giant, "So you are jealous, at least now we know".

Ade steps closer to the fuming fiery giant and enquires, "Who was this Bilikisu that you two are talking about and who is this so called brother of yours?"

Egbesu grins as he reveals Sàngó's long kept secret, "You see this great warrior who everyone knows for his stoic stance, also has a soft side".

Sàngó tries to stop Egbesu from letting his little secret out of the bag as he hushes and shushes the giggling mate but the war deity seems to be having so much fun exposing Sàngó's soft side. He continues his tale, "Long ago a beautiful princess came from a far Country to settle in the prosperous town of Ijebu-Ode. Sàngó, who was then the king of the great Oyo Kingdom, heard of her unequalled beauty. Though he already had three beautiful and powerful wives, he greatly desired this stranger, who was rumoured to be the daughter of the famous Queen of Sheba. She was called Bilikisu by the people of Ijebu-Ode, meaning powerful, yet gentle. Many kings and rich merchants sort her hand in marriage but the princess's wealth was greater than those of her suitors, who were always intimidated by her riches and power; but lover boy here would not take no for an answer. He persisted and pestered the beautiful Bilikisu until she agreed that the man she would marry must be the strongest in the land. Sàngó was confident to be that man because no man dared faced such a great warrior particularly one who commanded lightning and thunder; however on the day of the contest a huge and powerful warrior came from the east to challenge the favoured Sàngó; he too was a deity who, like Sàngó, controlled Lightning and Thunder from the sky, his name was Amadioha.

Size for size with well-matched supernatural powers, they fought on the ground and levitated in the air without a break or a moment's rest. The contest raged on for three days and three nights until it became clear that neither of the two love struck deities would succumb to the other. Since there was no victor, the beautiful princess declared the match a draw and didn't choose any one of the challengers. Ever since, Sàngó has considered the Eastern deity his foe".

After the startling revelation, Ade and his fellow heroes are dumbfounded while Sàngó marched ahead as he ordered the group, "We don't have time for this; we must get to the Four Gates of Virtue".

The others form a trail behind the long strides of Sàngó even as Egbesu's loud laughter fills the air.

The company walks for several hours, through solid grasslands and a soaking mangrove forest until they arrive at a plateau of moss covered low hills; there the leading giant decides that they should setup camp for the night to allow the human companions take a break from the long trek.

The two giants get tree trunks and branches, erecting a house frame which they cover with dried palm leaves; they also make soft sleeping mats for their human company from fresh grass.
Chief Kabaka starts a fire around which they all sit, feasting on a deer caught by the Samurai, Makato.

After the meal, the quiet mood is interrupted by Alex, asking an open question, "So how did all these start? I mean humans being put on the Earth, bad angels working to destroy the World and the good ones deciding to do their own thing. How long has all these been going on?"

Sàngó takes a deep breath then begins the tale known as, the history of all things.

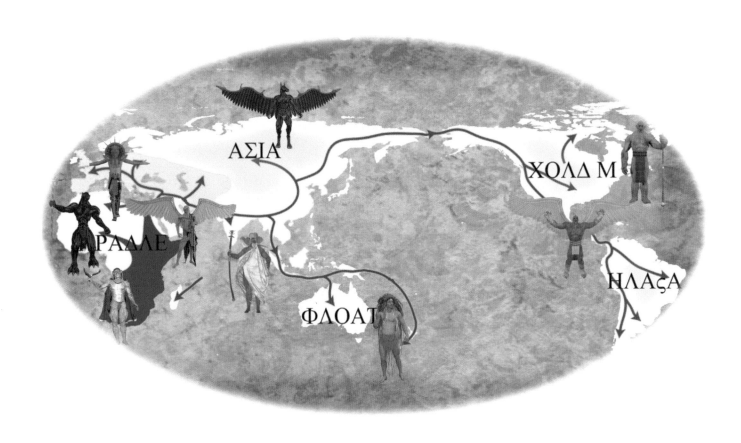

CHAPTER 9: THE HISTORY OF ALL THINGS

The History of All Things

àngó narrates history of all things;

The story I'm about to tell you was passed down to me through the long line of the descendants of the Celestial Guardians also known as The Watchers who bore mixed breed children with earthly women to produce supernatural, part angel and part human offspring. You here are the first people without angelic heritage to receive this knowledge in its pure form. There are things we know and there those that are hidden from us, for whenever the secrets of the Universe are revealed to man, the corrupted nature of man will seek to use the knowledge to dominate all that he has come to know. IN OUR BEGINNING, when all was void and time itself was unknown and unnecessary, came a voice in the emptiness and a Universe was created. It was without form and without life. From the voice came another whisper and many beings were made; they were the servant beings called Angels. These angels were created in many forms and hierarchy. There were those who served the Creator, the Almighty maker whose beginning and source was within Himself and from whom all life came. Another group of high angels were called to be guards of the throne of the Creator, and so it was that a sea of angelic beings emerged, each group immediately attending to what they were made to do. As the Creator whispered more words into the ears of the high angels, they themselves became lesser creators and their creations were brought before the Almighty, who saw them to be good and breathe life into the creations. Soon the endless void became populated by spheres, some dark and cold; while many burned with unquenchable flames as they shot far into the void, dispersing themselves as if to an appointed location. More colourful spheres were then created and were assigned to move in synchrony with the burning spheres; these were the first Worlds and they were without life. All these things were created with the authority of the Almighty and He saw that they were good. Over a period; billions of years as we now know it, though only a moment to the creators, many of these Worlds and spheres began to merge, exploding with the force only a supernatural can endure; with each collision giving birth to a new World.

Soon a natural order was formed and many groups of new Worlds revolved around its parent World. Of all the Worlds that were formed, one stood out; as it cooled, it formed itself into a glowing blue giant ball, yet tiny in the vastness of the space it revolved in; it was Earth. Earth was completely covered by a deep blue sea, which stuck to the surface of the young World as it spun around its own axis and revolved around a much bigger burning sphere; that which is now known as the Sun. The Almighty separated the sea from the firmament and made land to rise from the sea. A group of the creator angels were then sent to Earth to make creatures big and small, in the sea and on land; even in the sky were new creatures of glowing colours and textures. All these creatures had their own distinct voices which soon filled the entire new World producing a harmony that was pleasing to the Almighty and the Almighty liked it.

The lesser creators rallied around the Almighty and they sand His praise and music of the Celestial choir filled the entire Universe causing all living beings to worship the majesty of the God Creator. The Almighty God saw that all was good yet incomplete. God desired a different kind of creature, one which he could fellowship with, a special group who he would call His children; and so He commanded the lesser creators to make a new being which would look like God himself. So, man was made from the dust of the Earth, lying still on the floor and then God breathe into man's nostrils and he awoke. Many Men and women did they create and they moved around in pairs, man and woman hand in hand did they move and God saw that it was good and He liked it. With the mankind being the last creation of God, the Almighty returned to His heavenly throne and He rested.

God would often come down from the high throne of the upper Heaven to the growing and slowly maturing Earth, whose natural evolution and company He enjoyed. God came regularly to the middle of the Earth to the land now called Africa. Among the first Men and first Women that God created, was a couple who was later referred to as Adam and Eve. No one knows why God loved this particular pair so much but it is said that their pure love was so strong; it drew the Almighty to them; for it was from the essence of this force of love that they were created. God then made a garden, there he put Adam and Eve and blessed them to flourish. The garden became God's favourite place and He would often come to fellowship with them.

Over time there was a murmuring amongst the higher angels; it was a new aberration, it was a force opposite to that which the Almighty possessed and radiated. Eventually, God's great love for mankind created a deep envy in the hearts of the high ranking Angel, Lucifer the morning star who foresaw that man would one day rule over the World and even the angels. His jealousy was so intense that he caused a host of other angels in heaven to revolt against the will of God. The revolt was put down and the rebels were cast down away from the heavens and scattered all over the Universe. Most of these rebellious beings were entrapped by their own flame, and shone as gigantic burning orbs, banished from the Earth and lost among the stars.

Over time Lucifer learned how to control his anger, harnessing its power to move around all over the Universe, him and a handful of his leading rebel angels rode on a giant Asteroid which they steered and crashed into the far side of the earth causing a cataclysmic shockwave which wiped out most life on half of the World. The larger animals that lived along the edge of the continent were killed immediately by the blast while the smaller ones who lived along the dried out rivers died out of starvation. Whether by the will of the Almighty or whether because they were far away from the site of the blast, the human pairs survived. The earth-shattering blast also cracked the land mass of the Earth breaking it into several parts and over many ages the new lands began to drift apart, forming new smaller continental lands. Lucifer vowed to destroy God's most loved children thus proving that these children did not deserve such elevation from the Creator. Lucifer could not kill any of God's children directly because he lacked the authority neither did he possess the power to consume their essence, the prince of darkness, as he was later known; however swore to corrupt all that was good in these beloved children of God; so whenever God was away, the evil angel would visit the garden where God's favourite couple dwelt. Among the diversity of trees in the garden; which the Creator gave His charge to the couple to tend; the couple could eat all but two were forbidden to them; one was the Tree of all Knowledge which glittered with many stems towering tall above other trees but dropping back down like a weeping willow, bearing lots of diverse glowing fruits and The Tree of Life which stood by itself; its translucent stem pulsating at the misty core like a lustrous smoke; far away from every other tree for no other tree could withstand its glory; its light could be seen from every angle of the garden.

Disguising as a friendly animal inhabitant of the garden, the evil angel plotted to win the trust of the young couple. After a very long age of fraternizing with the unsuspecting pair, he offered to them one of the many glowing fruits of the sacred tree of all knowledge which was not yet appointed to them to partake, for they were not yet ready to receive any part of its intense knowledge. First, the false angel, in his slithering serpent form fed the forbidden fruit to the female who in turn fed the same fruit to her husband. Immediately the couple tasted the tabooed fruit, its power filled their immature minds and their nudity was revealed to them and they felt naked and they hid and covered their nakedness. Their transgression filled the air, drawing the attention of the Almighty.

Saddened by the disobedience of His beloved children, the Creator rebuked them and separating the sinned couple from the foul serpent, He put an enmity between its seed and that of the woman till the end of time. For their own part of the sin, God banished the man and his wife from the garden and exiled them from the paradise, sentencing them to a laborious life of working the very ground from which they were created. God then stationed a winged angel, keeping the man and woman away from returning to the garden. God also caused a flaming sword to revolve back and forth, guarding the Tree of Life; preventing the man and his wife from partaking in the second sacred tree, which would give them eternal life, effectively giving them godlike everlasting existence yet, now without the required purity to endure its power.

The devil then mocked God, saying, "Are these the children whom you loved so much more than we who laboured to create them? We, the angels are more worthy of your love and power than they who are mere mortals".

God's judgement upon the grinning serpent was swift and immediate, with a curse that turned the erect dragon-beast into a slithering, belly crawling snake. But God's love of His children was so great, He promised to redeem them of the corruption so that one day His fellowship with them will be restored.

Arrival of the Watchers

Over several ages as humans began to multiply in their great numbers across the land, God sent a group of Watcher Angels to the world; their duties were to teach the humans the ways of the Almighty and help them understand the nature and resources of their environment. The wise celestial beings were also instructed to keep the race of men away from the lurking evil fallen angels who were defeated and vastly dispersed after the great war in the heavens.

At first, the Watchers were good, guiding men in God's righteous ways but over time they began to lust after the beautiful women amongst the people they led. They married the fair women and their wives bore them offspring; a mixed race of supernatural beings; many were giants with exceptional knowledge and strength .

The Watcher angels and their extraordinary children taught humans many great crafts in building and agriculture. Sadly, the Watchers themselves grew eager to dominate the World and so they began to teach humans the ways to dominate and of oppression and warfare. Many warring groups soon formed and the people could no longer live together peacefully as one nation.

One by one each ruling Watcher angel gathered his own group of people; hundreds and some, thousands from the cradle continent to other parts of the Earth, establishing great kingdoms of demigods and men in far away lands.

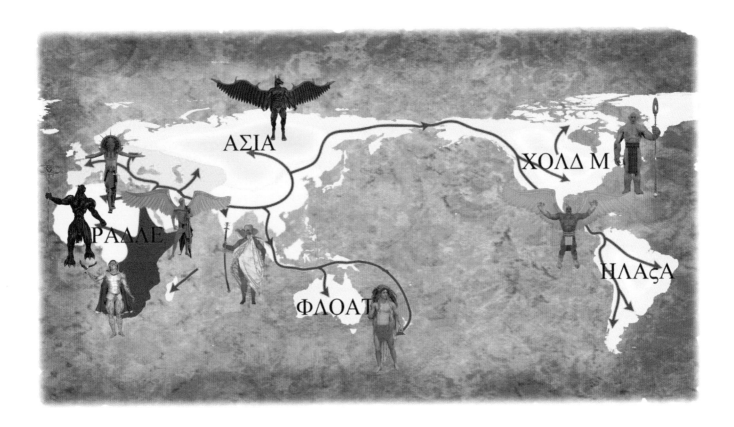

Some moved to the East, towards the great mountains then splitting into two groups.

One group pressed on to form the mountain tribe of present South Asia, where they cultivated new crop species and fabrics made from animal skin.

The other group trekked for generations to the ice country of the North; there they established great cities and kingdoms, eventually becoming very resourceful, learning how to survive the extreme cold region. They devised new warring tools and machines and also prospered, establishing trade with other peoples.

Several groups migrated far north to the land now known as The Middle East where they flourished for many generations but soon began to segregate due to competition and dominance by stronger communities, causing the prosperous Kingdom to split further into dozens of smaller colonies. The ways of these new societies became more diverse as their cultures changed. A few of these oppressed communities retraced their origins and migrated back to their homeland forming new groups in present day West Africa.

The populations that remained in the Cradle land, flourished upon the richness of the blessed land where extreme weather such as Earth tremors and sweltering volcanic terrains was absent. The rich land was also devoid of tsunamis, hurricanes, winter and ice storms so food supply was in abundance, requiring little or no human cultivation to flourish. Here also, a rich civilization grew and spread all over the vast land. Over time all the immigrated peoples of the world established trade relationships with one another; still segregating and forming new tribes as we have it today.

The Great Sin

As the peoples of the World increased in population and developed in their skills, they became corrupted by their own creations and began to make gods of men and objects, forcing others to abide by their new religions. Priests emerged as the custodians of these new practices and they became the self-appointed representatives and interpreters of these ever increasing idols.

The deviation of the celestial guardians and the people gave opportunity to Satan's fallen angels to mingle and even corrupt these newly formed kingdoms, preparing for a final destruction of all God's beloved children and creation. These foul angels, also knowledgeable themselves gradually influenced the rulers of each kingdom to turn to their foul ways and devious teachings. Sharing some of their own extraordinary skills and knowledge, they helped Kings and Princes of men defeat their competition and seize their treasures. Over time, various races of humans evolved, each race claiming superiority over others. Countries began to focus mostly on forcefully taking the foods and treasures of rival countries as well as abducting the peoples of other countries. Men and women were taken against their own will, some were even captured and enslaved by people of their own tribe and culture, turning them into unwilling human workforce and fighters at war, many were used to appease their new gods, offering the humans as sacrifices to their new false deities and lords.

The peoples of the World forgot who they were and where they came from. They forgot the Lord their God and turned away from His light and His love. They lust after the earthly treasures given to them by their new gods who taught them abominable ways to pleasure themselves. People no longer repented for their transgressions, instead were celebrated and rewarded for developing and promoting new ways of defiling their previous holy ways. The divine essence of music was desecrated; instead it became the very instrument for spreading the foul messages of their new demon gods. Freedom was given a new meaning and everyone was encouraged to live their lives without any inhibitions, claiming that there was no creator of man; instead that man became himself when the Universe became itself. Fornication and adultery were no longer seen as immorality but an expression of love.

The Almighty was greatly vexed because He saw that mankind had chosen darkness over light, evil over good and the devil over Him.

God caused a flood to cover the World; covering every land even submerging mountains; washing away the unclean and the unholy in the World. The Creator spared the few people who held on to His holy teaching. He also spared various beasts on land, in the seas and in the air that also were free from the corruption of the World.

Most of Satan's demons were swept away, whether destroyed or imprisoned; no one knows. The seeds of the Watchers and that of their offspring; born out of the fornication with the women of the earth were also judged by the flood, for they too, though called the sons of God; were also swept away. All the kingdoms built by man were destroyed by the raging tempest. Only a handful of men and their faithful families survived.

Five of hell's fallen angels escaped by burying themselves deep in the core of the Earth. Also seven of the Watcher angels were sheltered; though no one knows how they managed to escape the wrath of God; perhaps they were spared because they had not fully completed their primary task of protecting the children of God.

Now running out of time, Satan targets mankind in all forms and ways. Knowing that judgment will soon come upon him and his followers, he is planning a major onslaught on the World. His five fiercest demons who survived the flood have returned. They have infiltrated the top hierarchy of man's organisations again and so have used their influence to establish control over many the World's resources. It is these five demons who have setup the five beacons in the five towns here in Africa, being the cradle of mankind. They are plotting to generate a force which will create a rift in the World's unseen protective shield. If they succeed, hell's army will be unleashed unto the peoples of the World; no place and no one will be spared.

That is why we must not fail; we must do what is necessary to stop them; even if it will cost us our lives.

After Ṣàngó's harrowing tale there is a long silence and the young heroes seem nervous.

Even the powerful war deity Egbesu is also unsure of victory over such formidable uncanny hell monsters; he doubts the success of their mission saying, "We can't take on all five demon lords at their respective locations, there's no time".

In his usual rumbling voice, Ṣàngó agrees with his demigod mate, "No, there isn't but to bring down a structure, you only need to take down the central pillar. Brutus is the lord of the fallen ones on Earth, so it is him we must stop. That is why we are here in Ogoni. This is where he will plant his beacon. If we destroy his beacon, all other four will fall".

Egbesu emphasizes his doubts, "That will mean that we determine his precise location; which I'm sure you know will be cloaked, hidden from plain sight".

The Oracle gives a glimmer of hope to the group, "That is why we must invoke the hunter spirit. Ibinabo is Ẹdụlẹ́; she has the power and authority to invoke the spirit of the Panther Watcher. Her mother has passed that power to her. She is now the only survivor of the Leopard clan. When she invokes the Panther spirit, she will possess the vision to see that which is hidden to the ordinary eyes".

Ade cuts in, "I want to develop the ability to use my mind over matter".

Alex cynically picks on his pal, "Well, if you don't mind, then it will not matter".

Egbesu is not amused by Alex's needling humour but welcomes it as a good trait as he concludes, "Well, humour is a good thing; it may help you keep fear at bay".

Ibi asks why evil has been allowed to thrive for so long and not destroyed since it was identified long ago.

The wise Priestess explains to her, "Evil is not a thing that you can vanquish. Like good, it is a chosen path, a choice of action that is taken; created with a free will, everyone must choose what path to follow. Sadly Lucifer, out of envy chose the dark path and his followers freely chose the dark path as well. We must be guided in our daily choices by the spirit of the Creator in each one of us. It is a spirit which radiates love and it is selfless and kind".

PART THREE:

THE GATES OF VIRTUE

CHAPTER 10: JOURNEY TO THE LOST WORLDS

Protecting the Celestial Weapons

After Ṣàngó's extensive tale, the team falls sleep. At dawn, The Oracle is the first to get up, her chants wake the others up, without wasting any time; the Priestess sounds the call to immediately continue with the long walk to the location of the gates of time; and so the company set out facing the rise of the morning Sun.

The group trot along for hours under the gentle morning Sun and even into the scotching blaze of the midday Sun. Ibi, who has been walking alongside the Priestess, calls out to the two giants, "The Oracle is old and cannot keep up with your pace".

Egbesu stops and kneels on one leg and offers to carry the aged Priestess, "You have watched over me for a century while I slept. It will be my honour to carry you".

The old woman sits on Egbesu's left forearm and grabs on to his huge biceps. Ṣàngó presses upon the group that they're running out of time. The two giants pick up the pace forcing the four heroes and Chief Kabaka to sprint along, three of their strides matching one of the towering giants.

They run for miles without any rest from Sun-up to midday, finally coming to a clearing, the middle of which is a circle of prehistoric monuments.

Egbesu puts down the Oracle who then leads the group into a concentric circle of eroded stone pillars. Within the ancient Stonehenge, are seven gateways, three of which have collapsed.

As the group walks through the stone circles, the Oracle enlighten the group, "Here we are, at the gateways to the unseen Worlds where old secrets were kept. Once there were seven gateways, created by the seven surviving Guardians of men. After the great flood only these seven Watcher angels were spared; knowing that they had fallen out of grace because of their transgression, and that they had lost the authority of the Creator to do battle with the five demon lords who had returned; each of the seven guardians took their heavenly weapons far and deep into the unseen Worlds to the righteous ones who had kept themselves true to the Almighty's laws. It was said that those celestial weapons were the only weapons that could destroy any heavenly beings such as the fallen angels and demons of hell.

Though no Watcher revealed his true name; they were called by the form they took or the power that they wielded; every new generation called them by a new name and so their true names remain unknown till this day. Knowing that the end of their time on Earth was near, they created seven pathways leading to the unseen realms of the chosen peoples, each Guardian taking his weapon to its new keeper.

They sealed the seven gateways behind them as they walk through, putting a curse on each gate so that only the pure in heart can open the gates, even so, if that Seeker fails to retrieve the heavenly weapon, he would perish, the gate would collapse and that weapon would be lost forever.

Many generations after the Guardian angels left our World, the enemies of man grew bold and evil spread unchallenged. Then priests of the Order of the Watchers sent three Seekers, true and pure in heart through three gates to the lost Worlds to retrieve the sacred weapons. One Seeker journeyed through the gate created by the guardian called Jötunn, the Frost Lord.

Another Seeker walked through the gate of Anpu, Usher of Souls, also called Anubis by later generations.

The third seeker braved through the gate of Gaṇeśa, also known as Lord, Remover of Obstacles".

Sadly, the Oracle added; those three mystical weapons were not retrieved. The three Seekers did not return and the gates collapsed, sealing the pathways to three of the hidden realms".

Chief Kabaka, pointing to the four standing gates, he tells the four heroes, "Now we are left with these four. Each one of you must journey through a gate to the Worlds beyond and retrieve the remaining weapons of power; if you fail, the war will be lost".

The Secrets of the Seven Gates

The Oracle continues her advice to the young heroes, "These four standing gates are believed to be the most challenging passages of the seven. They offer the four virtues of Faith, Hope, Love and Sacrifice. No Seeker has been found worthy to enter these gates".

Chief Kabaka interrupts the old woman, emphasizing, "I'm afraid the fate of your trials is not revealed to us but we believe that you are the chosen ones".

Alex asks the Oracle, "Do you think we can survive the tests that will be put before us and accomplish the task where as you have said, three Seekers have failed and died in the lost Worlds?"

The Oracle's responds to Alex's concern by explaining what she believes, "I cannot foretell what you will encounter on the other side of the gates but the rulers of old believed in trials by ordeal and those trials are usually a set of three; each trial more challenging than the previous. So, I expect that each of you will have to pass three tests before you get to the place where you will find what you seek".

Ade trying to scare Alex, he teases the nervous companion, "Everything in the forest wakes up and tries to devour you; from the venom injecting insects swarming all around you to the swamps with crawling huge serpents slithering through the thick fog covering the forest floor. You will have to swing from branch to branch in the seemly ordinary trees but which truly are not trees at all but forest beings who will try to grab you and reap you to shreds if you linger too long at any one spot..."

Ade's prank gets to the already jumpy Alex, who yells at his mischievous pal, "Stop it Ade, don't joke, I'm being serious".

Ade creating even more panic in his nervous friend's mind, he continues his creepy tale, "Who's joking? You must remember that I won't be there to hold your hands, neither will Ibi be there fighting off the violent angry ghosts roaming through the dimly lit forests".

Alex protests, "It's easy for you to be calm, you are in your elements here and know how to handle yourself in awkward circumstances and I'm sure you know how to navigate through even the thickest of jungles. I wish we didn't have to go separately into the gateways".

The old Priestess cuts-in to the duo's conversation, dismissing Ade's prank threats, "The trials of the seven gates are not like any other. Victory against creatures of old is not determined by experience or strength but by the will of God, and of course the wisdom and purity of heart of the Seeker".

Alex asks the old Priestess, "Just to be clear, you are saying that we should venture into an unknown World and face unknown ordeals, maybe even monsters from another era, yet we should keep our cool all through whatever is thrown at us, retrieve some prehistoric supernatural weapon and walk back through these gates?"

Ade cynically dares Alex, "What! Mystery man, are you afraid of a little adventure?"

Ibi sighs as she accepts the task. She eagerly asks, "So, what are we waiting for?"

Without saying a word, Makato marches boldly towards a gateway but he is quickly stopped by Egbesu, who cautions the impatient Samurai that each of them must be blessed before they enter the gateways. The war deity walks Makato to one of the gates. The Oracle also takes Ibi's hand and walks the brave girl to the blue gate. Similarly, Ṣàngó' grabs Ade's hand, yanking the cautious guy to the fiery gate. Finally, Chief Kabaka beckons to Alex and they both walk to the front of the sky gate.

Each of the four adoptive mentors begin to chant some inaudible incantations, then suddenly the four gates swing open, revealing the nature of the pathway.

Entering the Four Gates to the Lost Worlds

Ṣàngó calls to the spirit of the creator of the fiery gate, "Oh mighty Aganju, great Orisha, father of my ancestors and guardian of men, I present to you Adebọ̀wàlé, the young but bold warrior of men. Let your spirit guide him through the ancient path which you laid yourself. Lead him away from any evil and give him courage when he becomes weary. Lend him your thundering voice to scare off enemies and strength to endure the onerous task which lies before him. Let your mark be upon him so that the noble tribes in whose care you placed your heavenly weapon can recognise him as your chosen warrior so that he can bring hope to mankind once again".

AGANJU LORD

Ṣàngó then asks Ade to kneel before him. The Thunder deity then murmurs incantations and prayers over the appointed seeker. After the prayers, Ṣàngó cautions the hero, "Remember, let your own spirit guide you in your decisions for within your spirit lies also the spirit of the Creator. You must know when to spare a life as well as when to pause and let nature take its course".

Ade stands to his feet after the endearing words of his mentor. Finally, Ṣàngó concludes with a farewell greeting, "You will go well and return well".

Ade stands at the gate, waiting for his friends to receive their go order; he gazes into the misty red atmosphere inside which he must travel.

Egbesu signals his new protégé, Makato to kneel. Egbesu starts his speech with a warning, "The Moon gate is the most mysterious of all the seven. It holds many secrets and a weapon which does not come from the Guardian angels but promised to him. Now you must earn that honour before you can receive it. Though I know you are worthy of this task, I fear you already carry a burden in your heart. This is not the time for you to burden yourself with revenge, for only the meek can receive the weapons of the Almighty. The angel who laid out this path is A-nuka, also known by the people of old, as Anunnaki, the deity who is connected to Earth and Heaven. There were many like him who came as Watchers but they were consumed by the flood leaving only this great guardian as the last princely angel to lead us to the path of the most sacred weapon we hope to possess".

A-NUNA LORD

Egbesu then asks Makato to walk to the open gate and gaze into the starry sky and Moon within.

Raising both of his huge arms, the war deity calls of the spirit of A-nuka, "Oh princely angel and appointed guardian of the children of the Almighty, I call upon your spirit to become once again what you were created to be; the light that shines in the darkness, pointing the path our chosen Seeker must take. I present to you, Makato, son of Kishimoto, sworn defenders of mankind against the servants of the evil one. Though his steps are his, touch his heart so that he can become one with the holy ground which he treads. Let your voice calm the storms in the hearts of the creatures or beasts that may cross his path and let him get your divine favour whenever it is needed". Egbesu also concludes with the parting blessing, "You will go well and return well".

While Ade and Makato wait for Ibi and Alex to receive their anointing and prayers, the Oracle pulls Ibi close to herself. The Old Priestess places both hands on Ibi head as she prays, "Ibinabo, daughter of the Leopard tribe, I anoint you as a chosen Seeker of the sacred weapon of the heavenly Watchers. As you stand before the blue gate of the past, which no living man or woman has walked, you will not stumble. Your path will be made straight and illuminated. The spirit of your hunter ancestors shall journey with you. Ibinabo, daughter of the soil, child of the brave hunter princess, Ẹdụlẹ́, the Black Panther; your eyes will see as clearly as that of the Panther, your sprint will be as swift as the hunting Leopard. You shall not be afraid, you shall speak the language of the forest and your ears shall hear the voice of the heavenly weapon calling to you and leading you through the right path".

ẸDỤLẸ́ LORD

The Oracle instructs Ibi to walk towards the open gate and look into the uncharted wilds which lay before her. The Oracle then calls out with a shriek voice, "Lord Master of the forest, protector of all things that grow and guardian of mankind, I bring to you, one of yours, direct descendant of the Ẹdụlẹ́ clan, who themselves have been blessed by you over many generations. Here is Ibinabo, bearer of good news; may her name ring through the forest which she is about to journey through so that all beings big and small may know that your anointed one comes and they must lead her to her purpose. May she fulfill what no one has achieved, to go into the gates of time and return with the prize; the celestial weapon which you have kept safe for her to obtain."

The Oracle, like the previous two mentors, sends forth her young heroine with the final blessing, "You will go well and return well".

The three already blessed heroes wait at their gateways for their fourth companion to be anointed, so Chief Kabaka wasting no time calls out the name of the last Seeker, "Alexander, Defender of the people, now you must answer to the call to which you were named. Step close and look into the Sky gate which calls on to you to fulfill your destiny. Fear not but rejoice because you did not choose this path but it chose you. The guardian who laid this pathway is the Heru, also known as Horus, the angel of kingship and of the sky.

HERU LORD

He is the angel who came in the form of a falcon and giant man. They say that his right eye shines like the Sun signifying power and his left eye shines like the evening star, the Moon, signifying healing. I call upon the spirit of Heru, the Watcher sent by the Almighty himself to be a guide and guard to mankind. To you, Heru, I present to you, our Seeker who has been tasked to journey through your gateway. Shine your Moon eye to illuminate his way so that he may not lose the path and when in trouble, blind his enemies with your Sun eye so that no harm will come to him. Carry him with your wings across treacherous rivers and deep valleys so that he can reach his destination unscathed and whisper into the ears of your chosen keepers of the heavenly weapon so that he may obtain that which he has been sent to recover."

Chief Kabaka then point into the sky gateway as he sends forth his anointed Seeker, "You will go well and return well".

The four anointed Seekers stand at the entrance of the gates to the lost Worlds; their attention now solely fixed on their gateway as if they await an order to proceed.

One by one the brave seekers turn around to one another bowing in reverence and communicating a farewell only by eye contact. From the distance, Ade and Ibi both gaze deeply at each other, completely entranced in a brief magical moment and a whisper of "I love you" between the two young lovers echoed in the complete silence which envelops the air; then Ade gives a thumbs up to his three fellow Seekers. The others respond with corresponding thumbs up, then as if performing a rehearsed recitation, they proclaim in unison, "There are things we know and there are things we don't know, but now we go see for ourselves".

Ṣàngó gives the go call, "Go, be whom you were born to be".

As the four take their first step into their individual doorway, each traveler is immediately sucked into a vortex. They disappear into the foggy atmosphere and the four gates instantaneously slam shut behind them.

Each of the four Seekers, encased in an air bubble which can be likened to the protective sac of a mother's womb, travels in their own vortex at a speed faster than light itself. They emerge in a boundary-less space of an expanding Universe; zooming past billions of Solar systems and millions of vast galaxies as if searching for particular planets. All around the infinite space, the overwhelmed travelers see millions of tiny bright lights far in the distance, some moving very fast like shooting stars while most jet slowly with a dim glow. They can see other lights, which seem to be fading out and do not move at all. When the bubbles of the four seekers come close to these lights, they can see faces of people. The bright lights have faces which appear to be happy but the stationary fading lights show faces that look frightened.

Suddenly the bubbles move or are steered to distant planets which far away appear as little dots in the vast space. As they get closer, the heroes see clearly that they are being taken to planets that look habited. Each bubble finds its predetermined destination and lands roughly, spitting out its passenger.

CHAPTER 11: FACING YOUR FEARS

The Ancient Leopard Tribe

Ibi's vortex lands her on to a thick bed of dried leaves in a terrifying forest whose trees are covered with very dense foliage. The nervous traveler struggles to meander through the tropical jungle; stepping over the expansive root lattice of the mangrove rainforest. She clings to the flexible stems of the thin trees and shrubs, desperately avoiding the creepy looking fern covered marsh land. The lone heroine charts a new pathway in the unexplored jungle. After a long exhausting trek through the musty forest, she comes to a mud hut with a thatched roof within a grassy clearing. On the front cracked wall of the circular hut are etched Roman letters *V III*; she is distracted by the sound of paper rustling behind her; a piece of parchment paper being blown around in the gentle wind catches her attention. She takes a few fast strides and steps on the paper; she grabs the tattered paper then shakes off the dust to see what is written on it. In bold letters a single word is printed, *SUBMISSION*. She discards the dirty paper and decides to head on to continue her quest; then she remembers the Oracle's words of advice, "You must purge yourself of the things of this World; you cannot pour water into a cup that is full already; open your heart to receive the grace from the higher kingdom".

She thinks to herself, "What has that got to do with anything here?"

She cautiously walks into the hut, shouting several hellos as she peeps into the open hut before finally entering inside. The tiny hut is uninhabited and without any household items except a long dust covered bench made from dried bamboo sticks. The exhausted adventurer decides to rest her tired legs and gather her thoughts, so she manages to blow off some of the dust from the bench. She sits down and as she contemplates her mission but she soon falls asleep. She is woken by a feminine whisper, sounding very close to her ears saying, "Call upon the spirit in you".

She suddenly springs to her feet, looking around, wondering if the voice is real.

The bold warrior undeterred by the strange environment and mystery voice, dashes into the lonely forest.

The inexperienced warrior wonders in circles in the confusing jungle for hours then she hears the gentle voice again, telling her to open her heart to the spirit of the Creator.

Ibi furiously shuts the voice up, arguing angrily, "Nobody could save my mother, not even the Ẹdụlẹ or God. I don't need anybody to protect me, I have looked after myself since childhood and I can look after myself now".

Suddenly, she hears the cry of a baby. She immediately stops her grumbling and races into the jungle, trying to follow the cry of the baby.

She sees a frightened little baby far ahead in the woods cornered by some green nasty looking creature. The vile creature steps slowly towards the crying baby ready to pounce on the helpless child. Ibi yells at the beast, "Get away from her, you vile coward. Face someone of your own match".

The creature turns its neck and head backwards, facing Ibi.

The green monster startled by the unexpected interruption, snarls at the female warrior and speaks mockingly to its challenger in a screeching domineering voice, "Be patient fleshy one, wait your turn, you look filling enough, let me finish with this appetizer before I devour you!"

Ibi growls angrily like a large cat as she warns the serpent-like beast, "I will server your ugly head from your slithering foul body before you even get near that child".

In a flash, the green monster jumps up, twisting in the air, it faces the challenger, ready to attack Ibi.

Both foes sprint towards each other, snarls against growls, ready to smash into each other for a fierce fight.

The green creature varnishes as they both collide; Ibi falls and rolls on the leafy jungle floor. She quickly springs to her feet and takes a fight stance, looking around the silent jungle, wondering where the beast is. She quickly turns towards the baby but the little child too seems to have just varnished. Instead Ibi sees carved markings on a tree at the spot where the child was. It reads again, *V-III* across and carved vertically is the inscription, ***SUBMISSION***.

The confused traveler stands still for a few minutes trying to understand what just happened. She questions herself, "Am I hallucinating? I'm sure I heard and saw a crying baby and a demon-like creature, or is the tension of this entire mystical adventure having its toll on me?"

The young adventurer can no longer shake off the seeming mirage and succumbs to the instructions of the unseen adviser. She falls to her knees and begins to sob, lamenting as she weeps, "Where were you when my mother needed you? Where were you when I was an unborn child, helpless in my mother's womb?

If you truly are the Creator of all things and the Almighty Lord of lords, why then did you forsake us? Now, here I am lost in a realm far from our World, unknown and uncharted. I don't know what to do, where to go and no one to lean on. If you love us as a father, as they say, then, please I need you now more than ever".

Ibi lies flat on the cold forest floor crying, feeling lost and despondent when she hears the gentle voice again, this time sounding quite close. Ibi raises her head up and is immediately blinded by a bright light. She covers her eyes with her arm, allowing just enough space to peep through. She sees a figure of a lady standing right before her, looking somewhat familiar, as if seeing an image of an older version of herself. The blinding light deems and Ibi slowly gets up, still staring at the lady, dumbfounded by what she is seeing, she asked the lady, "Are you my …"

Before Ibi completes her question, the gentle faced woman answered, "Yes, I'm your mother".

Ibi now crying tears of joy, rushed to her mother, clasping both arms around her in a gripping hug. Still speechless, her face beams with the brightest smiles she has ever had. She relaxes her hug but still holds on to her mother, determined not to lose her. Finally, she calms down enough to ask, "Are you really here or is this one of the tricks this place has been playing on me?"

Ibi's mother answers in the affirmative as she explains further, "I am not really here, but this is my essence. Your cries have been heard, and yes, our Father loves us immensely. It was he who saved you from the evil demon who wanted to stop your coming. My time had come and there was nothing anyone could do to stop it.

We do not know all ends, there are things beyond our understanding and control; we must always trust in the love that our Father has for us; never forget that. A great battle is coming and you have an important part to play in it. You are the Ẹdụlẹ, the Black Panther but you must acquire the weapon of the celestial watchers. They are the only weapons that can defeat the demons of hell; but you must pass the test put before the Seeker by the Guardians of old."

Ibi, still holding on to her mother begs her not to leave her again but her mother replies, "I will always be with you, as I have always been. I have watched over you all those years but you have been chosen for this task and you must fulfill it alone."

With her mother's assuring words, Ibi accepts her task but asks her mother one last question, as she fades away, "Will I see you again?"

Her mother's final words echo in the air as she fades away completely, "Surely we will meet again."

The Three Gates of Time

Ade's vortex tosses him out through the three-ring gates of time; they are the rings of the present, the past and the future. The determined seeker steps boldly into the unknown land. His gaze scans the strange land, glancing across the entire dimly lit landscape; carefully peering from far left to full right; beyond the immediate huge tall trees in front of him to the distant woods which fade into the misty land.

After satisfying his cautious self that no imminent danger lurks nearby, he carefully steps into the new territory. Ade's sharp eyes catch a pile of driftwood, in the middle of which are several short dried sticks, stuck into the ground. The upright sticks form two distinct Roman numbers, *V* and *IV* and lying on the ground by the side he finds an old scroll. Without any hesitation, he picks up the old delicate paper and carefully unfurls it. A single word is written on it in bold letters, ***REPENTANCE***.

Ade thinks about the word for a moment but can't make any sense of it. He drops the old dusty scroll and steps deeper into the foggy woods.

Suddenly there is a disturbing cawing noise of crows. A large murder of black crows flutter over and around Ade; he ducks here and there, trying to dodge the eerie birds; creating fear and panic in the adventurer that a bad fortune is coming his way. Ade's fear is justified when he notices a tall and monstrous object approaching his way. With nowhere to hide, the nervous seeker stands firm, feigning boldness. The huge object soon emerges through the thick fog and Ade notices a pair of monstrous chicken legs carrying a wooden house.

With long shaky strides, the approaching scary house tilts and rocks from side to side, staggering like a drunken man; looking as if it will topple over. Ade still stands his ground, knowing fully well that there is nowhere to run to.

The spooky house comes to a stop, still rocking like a pendulum, and then an old woman steps out in front of the elevated house. She speaks to introduce herself but she's interrupted by the young warrior; saying, "I know who you are, Witch! You are the infamous Baba Yaga".

Baba Yaga replies in a high pitch shriek voice, "Well then, that saves me the long boring pleasantries". The sorceress leaps from the high porch of the cottage and lands in front of Ade. With her face almost touching Ade's, she sniffs around his face and his back, like a hound smelling its prey.

Baba Yaga plays nice to Ade; she asks, "Since you know who I am already, be a gentleman and introduce yourself to me, so that we are no longer strangers but friends".

Ade is not so pleasant in his response, he replies Baba Yaga, "You are no friend of mine and I will not tell you my name. Be on your way and let me be on mine".

The old Witch giggles as she steps even closer to Ade; she finds Ade's cockiness amusing, replying, "Well, well, aren't we touchy? I just want one simple thing from you and I will be on my way and you on yours".

Ade and the Witch engage each other in a cat and mouse mind game, each one trying to conceal their disdain for the other.

Baba Yaga gets impatient and becomes more hostile as she accuses the Seeker, "You think you can deceive me? I know why you travel through here; I know everything. I control all that goes on in this realm; you are in my domain".

Ade answers, "I don't know what you are talking about".

Baba Yaga, yells angrily, "You are not worthy of what you seek. You have anger festering in your heart. You want revenge; revenge against those who killed your father and drove you away from your inheritance. You want them to surfer; I can see it in your heart; I can help you".

Ade replies calmly, "And why will you want to help me? I know want you want".

Baba Yaga responds, "You do? Then let's not waste any more time. Give me my most desired treasure; a kiss from a handsome youth".

Ade responds angrily, "I know what you are, Witch! I saw that movie. You know; the one where you kissed the lad and tried to suck his soul from him".

Baba Yaga grabs Ade by the shoulder, pulling him close as she brings out her drooling serpentine tongue, "Now boy, don't believe all what you watch on television. Television is bad for you. Now, come on, don't be shy boy; one wet kiss on my juicy lips".

Ade is disgusted by the old Witch's request; pulling away from the crooked Witch, he answers with a vehement negative, "I would rather die than kiss those slug slime rotten lips of yours. Besides I don't owe you any apologies for my revenge thoughts, as you say. I know in my heart that the Creator has already forgiven me and it is from Him that I ask for forgiveness".

Baba Yaga limps and reaches out to Ade, trying to grab the disgusted adventurer again. He pushes the raggedy Witch away; infuriating the determined sorceress. She screams in anger and laughs at the same time; her scream reverberates in the creepy forest; and her strange laughter sounds like alternating croaks of a frog and squeals of a Heron bird trying to cough out a fish stuck in its twisted throat.

The angry Witch curses and grunts as she threatens the bold traveler, "Now you shall know the meaning of fear. I shall entrap you in this realm for an eternity. You cannot escape me … you are mine!"

Baba Yaga starts to conjure a spell; generating sparks of lightning around the second gate of time.

Ade makes for a fast escape through the woods. Baba Yaga tries to chase after the energetic lad but her clumsy uneven wooden legs are no good for running. She curses and wails as Ade disappears far into the woods.

The Realm of the Dragons

Alex is tossed through a stone-ring portal on a rocky hill top into a barren World. The confused traveler looks up at the fiery sky and for the first time in his life, realises that no one is going to lead the way.

As he walks away from the encircling pulsating ring portals into the unknown land, he sees several inscriptions on one of the glowing rings which reads, *V-V HUMILITY.* He pauses for a moment wondering if that is a clue to where to go.

Without any leads, the young Seeker presses forward, looking around the bare landscape. He walks for miles, looking around the uninhabited patched terrain until he sees a line of hills far ahead. He makes for the hills, hoping to find a settlement of people and shelter but as he gets closer, he hears roaring sounds coming from the other side of the hills. The scared adventurer sneaks around the sharp corners of the hills, wondering where the terrifying sounds are coming from and what creature or beast lurks in ambush for him.

The still dazed traveler makes no sense of it. He looks around briefly, observing his new terrain then he begins his journey, running straight ahead as if he is sure of where to go.

He hears a thundering roar getting closer and with nowhere to take cover, the nervous traveler runs around the exposed hillside. The deafening roar gets closer, making the lone traveler panic even more. Alex finds an opening into a cave beneath the hill and immediately squeezes into narrow doorway.

The frightened traveler shudders inside the cave, hiding away from the monstrous creature making the frightening sounds. Alex lays quiet for some time, and then decides to explore the cavern.

He looks around inside the cave, hoping that he hasn't walked into another waiting danger. Suddenly he hears a voice inside the dimly lit cave but can't find who is talking. The nervous traveler is frightened even more when he sees a figure move within the cave wall.

A statue head in the cave wall comes alive and speaks, "Courage is not what one finds, it already exists in everyone. While some people discover theirs easily, some have theirs caged due to self doubt and others who have not truly found the need to release their real self, endure what is meant to be extinguished".

Alex summons a bit of courage and gets up; facing the huge sculpture head; he responds to the rock face, "You can talk?"

The stone head responds sarcastically, "Only when I'm talking to myself".

Alex drops back down and settles his bottom on a stone. The lone traveler buries his face in his palms, looking downcast, he talks to the cold rock, "Go on, say it, you won't be the first to call me a coward, spineless or whatever derogatory rude word you can muster; you'll be right. In fact I don't even know why I'm here, why I was chosen. Now that I think of it, I'm sure my role in this war is just to be used as bait, nothing more".

The rock head cuts in with a yawn and scolds the already beaten down explorer, "Now that I see you clearly, I don't think you are a coward at all. In fact, I think you are just lazy, trying to shirk your responsibilities. You want others to take on your task for you; it's what you've always done".

The stone head takes another long yawn, then continues his reproach of the already downcast young man, "Yes, that's it; and you know it yourself. Even at home, you hide within the walls of your house, always waiting for your father to step up to the problems. You let him face your family troubles alone; not helping out, instead you lay blame on the poor old man; no, you are not a coward, Alexander the not so great, you are weak!"

Alex is furious with the talking head, he picks up a rock and throws it at the immobile figure, yelling, "Ok, ok; stop already, I get it. Yes, you are right; though I think that's a bit too harsh; even coming from you, a stone cold sculpture".

The angry traveler pauses for a moment, bringing back the quietness of the cave.

He recollects himself and in a calmer tone he apologises to his talking figure, "I'm sorry; this has never happened to me before; actually, I don't think I've even gotten angry at anyone before; the only person I have ever gotten angry with actually, is myself".

The stone head apologises too, "I'm sorry too, this has never happened to me too".

Alex turns and facing the head, he agrees with it, "Of course is has never happened to you; you're a rock all alone in a cave; it never happened to you because you have never met anyone to vent your toxic anger on them".

They both laugh and joke around for a while, then the rock head tells the Seeker, "Your only problem is that you give up on yourself too quickly; I mean in your mind, you lose faith in yourself even before you try. You are not a coward, neither are you lazy but you must understand that when a task is appointed to you, only you can accomplish that task. Now you have been called to a mission and to achieve your goal, you must pass this trial. You have been lucky so far; you narrowly missed the first of two dragon brothers. You will encounter the other one on your journey; and as you know, dragons are very wise; they will try to trick you. Now go, be on your way and stand your ground against every foe you meet".

The head looks away and then out of guilt, looks at Alex again and says, "Err, let me correct that, you don't always have to stand your ground; actually, most times, you may want to run… or beg... Or…"

Alex stops him, "Yeah, okay, I get it; thank you. You have opened my eyes to see the wall I built over the years, in front of me. Now it is time to take down that wall".

The rock head begins to freeze back into a solid statue but it manages to utter its last words, yelling, "Beware of the two brothers".

The now worried adventurer races back and rubs the rock face all over; trying to bring it back to life but the head in the rock wall is already lifeless.

Alex speaks aloud to himself, "Why do they always do that. Why speak at all, if you are not going to finish what you want to say?"

Alex doubles his pace, racing through the narrow corridors of the cave.

The Forbidden Garden

The traveler's vortex transports Makato through the Universe, moving between various lost era and passing through unknown space before finally tossing him into a dark creepy forest.

The vegetation looks and feels tropical but the apprehensive traveler knows that this is no earthly jungle; he makes his way forward pushing through tightly packed crusty trees and a continuous web of ensnaring vines. Makato gently pushes apart the weeds and branches, showing reverence to the old jungle. After several hours, which feels like an endless time, the weary adventurer takes a rest. Leaning on a tree with a dry scaly bark, he soon feels the tree move. The apprehensive seeker turns around and comes face to face with a gnarly tree. The jerky tree turns around slowly as if wondering what bold mortal dares come before it. Soon Makato is faced with a real life breathing Iroko tree; the keeper of the forest, one of many sentinels of the hostile jungle. The large face of the forest guard spans across the huge stem and is longer than the height of the human. With a frown and a deep growl, the Iroko challenges the intruder, "Those who know me dare me not and those who provoke me have never heard of me, who are you to violate the serenity of the forbidden forest?"

The Samurai takes a bow before the impatient sentry and introduces himself, "I am Makato, descendant of the Kishimoto clan, protectors of mankind. I am one of four, chosen and sent to retrieve the ancient weapon of the heavenly defenders; for war is upon us all".

The angry Iroko pulls out its deep roots from the earth; some of which raise the already tall tree to even to a greater height; standing much taller, soaring over the mortal man. Iroko takes a swipe at the Seeker but the swift ninja ducks the twisting tentacle and stands back, still trying to convince his attacker that he comes in peace but the impatient forest guard continues its attack on the Seeker. Makato makes for the cover of the jungle, running deeper into the forest.

Iroko chases after Makato, clearing a path through the clustered rainforest, arousing the sleeping forest, waking many strange animals and beasts. Soon Makato realises that he is being chased by a bunch of hostile creatures. Running through the wild jungle and looking around and behind him, Makato trips over a root and takes a tumble. He recovers from his fall only to face another strange creature. With nowhere to run, the traveler is cornered by Iroko and his new adversary; a humanoid being; complete with long arms and legs, a moss covered torso and a stern face; Makato encounters Anjonu, another sentinel of the forbidden forest. The inscription *V-VI* glows for a moment on the new sentry's huge chest then fades away. Before Makato can utter a word, as if to hush the forest violator, Anjonu's deep baritone voice rumbles in the air, quoting a familiar phrase, "Only those who hunger and thirst for righteousness, will be filled!"

Sensing that the sentinels will not stop in their attacks, Makato escapes through a gap in the trees, running far; further into the mysterious forest.

Makato meets the serpent of old; the cursed snake of Eden; still possessed by the essence of the deceiver; it takes the Seeker to a comfortable place within the forest and shows the tired voyager a soft comfortable bed of scented roses. The slithering creature offers Makato food, drink and pleasures, enticing the overwhelmed human to abandon his mission and think of his own comfort; dissuading the adventurer, saying, "No single man can save an entire World, especially one that does not want to be saved".

The snake reminds Makato of the futility of the sacrifice of his parents and the avoidable suffering and loneliness Makato suffered as an orphan child and now the same orphan is thrown into a perilous forest, hunted by savage beings. The serpent urges Makato to feast and rest but the devoted traveler rejects the temptation of the ancient vessel of the fallen angel and he rebukes the snake for trying to sabotage the sacred quest.

Then the snake, not giving up, takes Makato to an enchanted cavern, there it offers to the Seeker, a pile of treasures; a collection of the finest gems and other precious items beyond what any man has ever seen. The snake raises its body high above the ground, its eyes peering into the human's, trying to hypnotize the traveler.

Makato rebukes the snake a second time; calling it by its master's name, Satan's vessel. Makato lays a curse on the serpent, "Oh ye traitor, who once betrayed the father of our fathers and mother of our mothers, the limbless reptile cursed by the Creator, impenitent and giving easily to evil; I, appointed hero of man hereby condemn thee by the power of the Almighty given to all born of a woman and a man; to an everlasting loneliness amongst all creations. You shall be cast out of all gatherings of animals and beasts of the land, sea and air; you shall be an enemy of all and shall be trampled upon by all till the end of time".

With that, the snake coils back into a hole in the ground and Makato continues on his adventure, seeking the weapon of the guardian angels.

The Samurai becomes lost in the confusing twists and turns of the jungle and soon finds himself face to face with the creatures that have been pursuing him.

Makato is surrounded by the band of irate strange beasts and enraged beings. They close any possible exit, trapping the exhausted Seeker.

Perplexed, Makato drops his defensive stance and falls to his knees, awaiting his fate. Just then the cornered traveler spots a lone animal sitting calmly, far behind the mob of angry creatures. Makato recognizes the white fox; it's the White tailed Kitsune, the supernatural protector of virtuous travelers. The gang of ferocious beings pounce on the helpless adventurer but finds that the trespasser has vanished. Makato is saved by the Kitsune, taken by its mystical power to a serene part of the forbidden forest.

CHAPTER 12: SECOND TRIAL

A Prerogative of Mercy

Ade runs in between the chicken legs of the Witch's house. Afraid to hit her own house instead of the escaping Seeker, Baba Yaga hesitates to cast a spell on him, giving Ade just enough time to get underneath the towering cottage. Ade tickles the chicken legs causing it to sway dangerously all around. The house giggles with a deep chuckle, twisting, turning and almost falling over. Ade escapes through the bushes, losing Baba Yaga in the commotion; who herself never dares venture far away from her malevolent cottage, the source of her witching powers.

Ade continues running for several hours until he runs out of breath. He soon realizes that the landscape has changed from the gloomy woods of tall trees into a hilly plain with a large lake. Ade trips over bones of long dead animals. Within the dried bone formation, Ade see another set of sticks buried in the ground; like the previous sticks, it forms the Roman numbers, *V-VII*, and next to it is a scroll. He quickly opens the scroll and it reads, *MERCIFUL*. Looking around the scattered bone formation, the stunned traveler notices that the bones are not of any animal he recognizes. Spanning great lengths, the main body is detached from a massive bone skull. It soon dons on Ade that Baba Yaga's spell opening the second gate of time, has actually merged the present age with the past; bringing a long lost primeval era of the dinosaurs to the present time.

The loud cry from across the waters takes Ade attention away from the bone skeletons. He hides from the monstrous beasts battling far across the lake. The frightened young adventurer observes the scenario for a while then realizes that the battle is an unfair fight; a mighty dinosaur has his legs entangled in a bunch of vines while his opponents; three Wormbeasts are getting the best of the king of the dinosaurs.

At first Ade thinks to himself that it is his chance to get away while the gigantic enemies are having a go at each other; but he then recalls the message of the last scroll. Believing that the message was put there for this moment and telling him to show mercy, Ade decides to save the outnumbered and incapacitated groaning Tyrannosaurus Rex.

Ade sneaks around the lake, getting close to the fierce fight, he hides behind a tree trying to decide how he can help the losing animal. The ferocity of the fight and the heart wrenching squeals and moans of the weakening dinosaur scares Ade as he gets close to the scene. He murmurs to himself, "How the mighty are fallen; then as he turns away, heading to the forest he catches a glimpse of the dinosaur's eyes, staring at him as if begging for help.

He freezes for a moment and shakes his head saying to himself, "I hope I'm not going to regret this".

He carefully navigates through the thorny bush, squatting as he gets close to the warring beasts, still talking to himself, "I don't believe I'm doing this."

The Wormbeasts drag the Trex even deeper into the water making it even more dangerous for Ade to get to the entrapping vines. He manages to get to the sinking dinosaur and begins to carefully pull the vines away from the animal's legs; occasionally docking from the view of the terrifying slime worms.

The hero whispers to the dinosaur as he pulls off the last trapping plant, "I know you don't understand one word I'm saying but I believe everyone deserves a second chance; I bring you hope".

The dinosaur stays still for a moment as if to give his saviour the chance to get clear, then in an angry twist the huge Trex springs to his feet and with a deafening roar, he bites through his nearest attacker, cutting it in half.

He grabs a second Wormbeast and shakes it violently in his powerful jaws like a canine shaking a venomous snake, preventing it from taking a shot at it. The third worm; seeing that it didn't stand a chance alone against the freed enemy quickly wriggles through the water, escaping to the other end of the lake.

From a safe distance Ade looks back at the giant lizard king tearing away the flesh and eating the lifeless Wormbeast. The daring seeker smiles, happy that he was able to save the dinosaur king. Ade continues his journey through the treacherous forest, evading many unsavory creatures along the way. Not actually knowing where he is heading, he finds himself in a swamp. Ade is buried knee length as he wades through the sticky marsh. It's a long and tiresome waddle through the massive wetland. As he pushes along, he begins to feel the absence of his other companions, especially his new found love, Ibi. Ade soon starts to feel the unpleasantness of being alone; a serene life he once desired; back in London, before the beginning of this strange adventurous life.

Talking aloud, not caring who or what may be hearing him, he questions himself, "It's funny how you get so attached to people who you once taught you'll be glad not to see. I can't believe that in just a few days, I can have such strong feelings for someone. I miss her now so much; I wish we are together now, eh, well… not in this swamp though".

The love struck adventurer pauses in the muddy soil, completely ignoring the buzzing flies all around him, feeling lonely and sad; then shaking himself to reality, he thinks to himself, "I just pray Ibi and the others are having it much easier than this".

Ade manages to drag himself out to dry land. He falls on his back to catch his breath when he hears distant voices, sounding like people but not exactly comprehensible. He pulls himself up quickly and without any hesitation he follows the sounds.

Suddenly Ade feels a gust of cold wind across his face; he immediately knows what that means. Grumbling with fear, "No, no, no; this cannot be happening again. That crazy old witch must have opened the third gate of time". He hurries across the short grassy land ahead; on to a high rocky ground. He is frozen with surprised, his gaze fixed as he stands agape, staring ahead.

The Value of a Pure Heart

Ibi cannot stop thinking of her mother as she races through the magical forest. Her legs become wary from jumping over high rocks and her hands and knees become sore from crawling through narrow tunnels and tearing through entangled vines along the long winding trail. Even a dogged adventurer like Ibi eventually succumbs to the reality of hunger and thirst. Ibi rest on a fallen tree, catching her breath and looking around the nearby bush for any wild fruits or seeds she can eat. Deeper into the thick bush, her eyes catch a cluster of smooth stem trees, which look like guava fruit trees. The tired explorer musters her last strength and pushes through the thick bush to the tree cluster. To her disappointment the guava trees do not bear any fruits at all, but Ibi's hunger is temporarily forgotten as she notices carved writings on the smooth stems of the trees. The markings are similar to the ones she saw previously, only these ones are different. On one tree are the markings, *V-VIII* and on the middle tree is written, *PURE*, then next to that is a third tree with the word, *HEART* carved into its stem; viewed together, they read, *V-III PURE HEART.*

Ibi is not amused, shouting as if talking to perceived stalker, she complains, "This is not funny, if you really want to play a treasure seeking game, at least pin a fruit on a tree every now and then!"

Suddenly a soft mango fruit drops on her head. She yells in pain and still complains even more, "You didn't have to do that! She listens for a response but there is no answer".

The hungry traveler hurries and picks up the ripe mango fruit and waits for a moment whether any more fruits will drop. Completely famished, Ibi sits down on the grassy ground. She wipes the soft fruit on her shirt ready to take a chunk out of it, but her meal is interrupted by a sad whining sound. Ibi sees a Vervet monkey sitting still and staring at her, without uttering any sound, its innocent eyes hypnotic enough to evoke a strong sympathy even in the hardest at heart. Ibi laughs cynically as she shakes her head indicating that she won't fall for those cute eyes, turning away to continue her juicy fruit meal; she sees a second pair of cute eyes peeping from behind the silvery-gray, black-faced monkey. Ibi soon realizes that they are a pair of mother and child. Ibi talks to the two primates not minding if they understand what she is saying or not, "I think you need this more that I do".

She tosses the mango fruit to the mother. The mother ape gently picks up the fruit and offers it to her baby. Waving to the feasting pair, the young traveler gets on her way. The baby and mother monkeys take turns as they take pinch size bites from the succulent fruit. Ibi takes a deep sigh and murmurs, "That's that then!" Ibi's long lonely walk soon begins to have a toll on the tired and hungry traveler. Whether it's the hunger and exhaustion caused by the tiresome journey, or an illusion created by the mysterious forest, Ibi begins to see things. She sees Ade running towards her; arms stretched, reaching to embrace her. Ibi smiles and she also races towards her true love. They both clasp each other in a prolong hug, kissing and laughing; then as immediate as the vision of Ade appeared, it quickly vanishes. Ibi is confused; she runs around the plain, calling out to Ade; she turns clockwise and anticlockwise looking for her love. She falls to the ground and begins to cry, and then she hears Alex calling to her, telling her to stop crying. Alex grabs her hand and pulls her up to her feet. She kisses Alex on his cheek and tells him that she's so glad to see him. She asks Alex if he knows where Ade has gone, telling her childhood friend, "Ade was just here a minute ago".

She turns around again to see if Ade is behind her but she doesn't see him. She turns back to Alex but he too is not there. Ibi then realizes that she is daydreaming. She shakes off the trance and a sense of fear hits her as she begins to worry that if she is already delusional during the day, she wonders what will happen if she doesn't leave the enchanted land before nightfall. It suddenly dawns on her that the jungle is not a place to be in the dark of the night, who knows what ungodly creatures lay hidden, waiting for the cover of darkness to attack and what manner of prey will they be stalking, hope not humans. Now working against time, she crosses the grassland but finds herself in another jungle. Though not as scary as the past forest, it didn't have any trail either. She snaps a dry branch off a nearby tree and using her new tool, she clears a path for herself. Taking one bold step after another the lone explorer ventures further into the new jungle. Without warning, it starts to rain; it is as if a huge river is flowing from above. With no refuge from the torrent, the distressed adventurer doubles her pace, swinging her clearing stick in front of her, creating a pathway for herself. Soon Ibi notices that a stream of water starts forming underneath her feet; flowing along with her, washing along the loose clay soil of the slopping ground. Before long, Ibi finds that she is caught in a high speed mudslide.

She tries to grab the seemingly passing tree branches just as she struggles to remain upright, while being pushed down the slope by gravity. She trips over a tree root on the ground and takes a tumble in the nature formed channel.

Ibi tries to protect her head from being smashed into rocks and roots while being swept along the forest muddy ground when suddenly a thick vine drops down from a tall tree. Amidst the tumbling and slides, she spots the jungle rope far ahead in her path. She reaches up on getting to the vine and grabs on, pulling herself up clear from the raging flood beneath her; waiting for the flood to pass.

When all becomes calm, she sees the mother Vervet monkey up at the end of the vine; it was she who dropped the jungle line which saved Ibi. One after the other more black-faced monkeys emerge from the shadows of the jungle and soon a large group of monkeys start to hoot; cheering the brave seeker, celebrating her survival. They lead her to their home in the jungle; where a whole troop of monkeys queue bringing lots of fresh fruits to the tired traveler. Ibi looks up to the heavens, relieved to be unharmed, she prays, "Thank you, Lord".

After Ibi is filled and rested, the mother Vervet monkey leads Ibi from the community of silver-gray monkeys, through the rainforest to the edge of a grass plain. The matriarch monkey hops and hoots as she points her guest in the direction out of the jungle.

Ibi hugs the fluffy primate, and they both hold on to each other in a long embrace. Finally, they let go and then walk in opposite directions; one heading home, while the other continues in her quest.

The Reward for Peace

Alex navigates through the labyrinth of the cavern of the talking head and comes out into a desolate land. The land is scotched; the trees are dead and there is no grass. It seems like something had burnt the life out of the land. Alex finds a set of travel ring portals ahead; as he tries to enter the rings, hoping to exit the desolate realm, he sees another set of inscriptions on the front ring; this time they read, *V-IX*, with the word *PEACEFUL* written after.

Without warning Alex is confronted by a brown dragon. The beast lands directly in front of the defenseless traveler, cutting him off from any escape route or retreat.

The dragon immediately challenges Alex to a duel but Alex knowing that he is no match for the flying beast, kindly refuses, claiming that they should be acquainted with each other better so that the victor may know who he has defeated.

The impatient dragon insists that they can get to know each other during their combat; by their strength and weakness; so there is no need for talk. He threatens the human traveler, swinging its stout tail across, trying to sweep its weaker opponent off his feet. The scared Seeker runs around, using the dead trees as obstacles between him and the attacking dragon.

Alex tells the belligerent dragon, "You have been trying to get me to fight you but I'm not going to fight you; you are not my enemy. Why should we fight and separate our powers when we can unite as companions and have greater strength?"

The dragon too proud to fight an unwilling adversary, decides to try another trick.

The beast pleads, "Dear warrior, I have a little itch on my back and I cannot reach it. Can you please scratch it for me?"

Alex replies, "Ah, nice trick. If I come close, you will eat me, no thanks".

Again the dragon calls out to the unwilling opponent, "Hey, young warrior, my hands are too short and I haven't been able to reach my mouth to feed myself for a long time now, feed me so that I may not starve".

Alex is suspicious, querying the beast, "Another trick of yours. If you can't feed yourself, how have you been eating all these while?"

Dragon answers, "I'm afraid, my helper is no more, he smelled too nice and I couldn't resist the urge of a little bite".

Alex, disgusted; yells, "What! A little bite of what?"

The dragon replies with a grin, "I asked for a leg but he misunderstood and gave me his head. I guess leg and head sound alike".

Alex now afraid, probes further, "So you ate him?"

Dragon laughs as he continues, "Ok, smart guy, you tell me how you will help to feed me".

Alex, not finding it funny, becomes cynical, "Why don't I throw the food and you catch it in your mouth, how does that sound?"

The Dragon, now not finding Alex's response amusing, growls, "That sounds insulting. Do I look like a puppy dog to you, that you play fetch with?"

The adventurer plays it cool by asking, "Okay, how about you just bending over your meal and eating it like a normal Dragon?"

The surprised Dragon agrees, "Oh, I never thought of that, it does sound crude and uncivilized though, but feasible. Let me try that. You hold the food in your little hands for me then".

Alex refuses, "Not a chance. Do you think I'm stupid?"

Dragon teases the human, "Actually, I was hoping that you were. You do know that you can't leave here alive. How will that look for my reputation? If I let you pass, It will seem that I am beginning to be soft… err, and I don't mean a soft skinned, you know; but my brute side; and other explorers will think that I have become nice and weak".

Alex continues, "I promise you, I won't say anything to anyone about you letting me through. I will tell them that I played dead and because you are a majestic being of honour, you don't eat scavenger's food; so you stepped over my presumed corpse and walked away".

The altercation continues and soon the two adversaries become engaged in a war of riddles. Alex knowing that use words is not his strongest attribute; thinks of a way to evade the intelligent creature's trick questions.

In its rumbling voice, the dragon asks the young Seeker, "By the way, what is your name and why does your path lead you through my territory?"

Alex replies the flapping beast, "Do all dragons ask the same questions?"

The cunning dragon goes again with a follow-up question, "Of all places in the Universe, what destiny has brought you to my land?"

The calm explorer replies, "Are there treasures here to be guarded, why have you nested here?"

The dragon, taken aback asks, "All who have travelled through this realm tremble before me; aren't you afraid of me?"

Alex answers, "Are you here to protect something or prevent trespassers?"

Determined to get the simple trespasser of guard, the dragon continues his grilling, "Do you know how many seekers of fortune have fallen before me?

Alex calmly responds, "Why? Do you have supernatural powers?"

Now getting worked up, the winged beast presses on, "Do you know what it's like to be trapped in this desolate realm?"

Sensing some hostility from his foe, Alex replies, still with his own question, "Do you despise your kip, which I must believe is a glittering bed of gold?"

The infuriated Dragon then rumbles, "Why do you answer all my questions with another question?"

Alex pretending to be naïve, replies, "Why are you getting so angry?"

The dragon becomes enraged, pounding the dry dusty ground as it stomps towards the still calm man. The dragon asks him, "Why are you answering every question I ask you with another question of your own?"

But the gentle traveler replies again yet with another question, "Why do you keep asking a question when you can tell me about yourself; show me how great you are; your triumphs and conquers?"

The dragon falls for the wise traveler's flattery; it proudly obliges, "Yes, you are right, why will I; a magnificent conqueror condescend to talking to an insignificant wimp like you?"

The over-confident serpent spins around; its huge body clearing the ground around it, churning up a cloud of dust, then settles down in a comfortable pose. Alex observes the beast as he behaves like a dog performing the ritualistic round turn before lying down then it occurred to him that this terrifying creature, after all, is just an animal.

He tells the arrogant dragon, "Before you start your engaging tale, I want us to play a little game".

The dragon replies, "Games? Are you trying to trick me?"

Alex calms the creature, "No, no, no, I dare not. I just want you to show me some of your qualities so that I can see for myself, how true whatever tale you are going to tell".

The unsuspecting dragon agrees for just one game and then Alex picked up a stick and tells the dragon, "I'm going to throw this stick as far as my strength can toss it and I will count to see how long it will take you to retrieve it".

The dragon laughs and agrees to the challenge, telling his opponent, "You forget that I can fly, I will retrieve your little stick before you count to three".

Alex flings the stick far into a bush. The dragon springs up into the sky and dives straight into the bush to get the stick but soon discovers that it's not just a cluster of weeds but an entanglement of thorny vines. Trapped in the web of creeping plants; each torn tearing the wing membrane of the serpent; the dragon realises that it has been tricked. Cursing and yelling as it gets pricked; the angry beast knows that he has been incapacitated.

Alex hurries into the ring portal and he is immediately transported away from the barren land.

The Burden of Devotion

The white tailed Kitsune transports Makato to the edge of a stream within the forest; away from the chaos and Makato finds himself alone with the white fox. He shows reverence to the ethereal fox, bowing and thanking the supernatural creature for rescuing him. Then Kitsune causes a white smoke to appear in the air, spelling *V-X* and the word ***DEVOTION***. After the smoke clears, she warns the seeker that the mission may cost him his life but the Ninja answers that he will gladly give his life to the noble cause of ridding the world of evil, especially one that has robbed him of his parents. The Kitsune tells him, "You must endure the Way of Sorrows for it is only those who are ill-treated because of their honesty that will triumph over the evil of this World".

The Ninja takes a deep breath and looking into the Mystical fox's blue eyes, he commits to the ultimate trial, answering, "I am ready".

The white fox counsels the Samurai further, saying, "To prove your righteousness, you must unburden yourself of the distractions of the World. Your journey here will test your patience and your humility. It is only your devotion to your quest and commitment to stand against all evil that will strengthen you during your ordeal".

The Kitsune sends forth the brave seeker, waving its white fluffy tail, sending a strong vibration into the air, and then she reveals her true status by separating her other eight hidden tails which were tucked into one all this while. Makato is shocked as he now realises that he has been honoured by being in the presence of the mythical thousand year old nine tailed Kitsune. He takes a bow, and then sets out bravely into the hostile forest ready to face his test; he looks behind him at the White fox, but she is no longer there.

Makato is immediately snatched by several long forest vines and roots shooting at him from within the dark forest. The Seeker does not resist the tug as he is pulled into the jungle. The recoiling vines fling Makato into a soggy marsh field, infested by biting bugs. There he is surrounded by his bizarre hunters.

The huge Iroko sentinel presents the intruder to be judged. The irate forest mob yells repeatedly, "Reap him apart, reap him apart!"

Then the tall sentry, Anjonu announces Makato's sentence, "You are hereby judged guilty of violating the sanctity of our realm, the forbidden forest; you shall be put to death".

The multitude of vicious creatures descends on the compliant Seeker. They beat, scratch and toss him around then they tie a rope around his neck. He is dragged through the dank forest, calling out all dwellers and showing the traveler as the foretold desecrator who will one day reveal to the World, the hidden location of the garden of paradise; which they have protected since it was proclaimed forbidden to all humans and beasts. The multitude beat the captive to stupor and they flog him back to consciousness three times as they parade him through the forest until finally he collapses and all lashing doesn't get the prisoner up. The faithful Seeker takes his punishment willingly; not resisting or fighting back; instead remains meek and steadfast to the quest, ready even to give up his life for the divine mission.

Hearing that the sacred garden is located within the forbidden forest, Makato pleads with the fierce mob to take him to the gate of the legendary earthly paradise planted by the Creator Himself, so that he can gaze upon the work of the Almighty before he is killed.

The murderous crowd is vexed even more, deciding to kill the trespasser on the spot but the sentry, Anjonu restrains the angry gathering. The tall humanoid lifts up Makato and takes him to the gate of the forbidden garden to fulfill his final wish. He drops the Seeker, who collapses like a ragdoll on the ground.

A whooshing noise encompassing the forest wakes the barely conscious traveler. The angry multitude is scared back by flames of the speeding encircling blazing sword flashing its scorching trail of fire around the perimeter of the sacred garden; forming a hurricane of fire in the forest. Mustering his last ounce of strength, Makato lifts his head and smiles as his eyes perceive the fabled blazing sword.

CHAPTER 13: FINAL ORDEAL

A Final Farewell

Ibi is in a pensive mood as she strolls over the peaceful meadow outside the border of the mystical rainforest. She contemplates the surreal events she endured to get to this point. After the grass plain, she comes to the bank of a river. The water is clean and seems shallow and safe enough to wade across. "But first, I have to wash off this red mud and sweat from my body", she tells herself.

She dives happily into the river, washing and scrubbing the thick mud from all over her body, hair and clothes. She decides to stay longer in the river and allow the gentle waves relax her tensed nerves. As she lies afloat in the fresh water, she again remembers her dear Ade and she longed to be with him. Looking over the horizon, Ibi observes the beautiful sunset; she watches it for a while then reminds herself that this is not a pleasure trip and it will be getting dark soon; so she gently wades across the stream. As she steps out of the water she hears a sound of someone or something in distress in the river. The energetic lady runs along the river bank, looking up and down the slow flowing stream; then she spots a Leopard cub struggling to stay afloat midway in the water; its little paws too small to grab on to a moving log in the water. Ibi immediately dives back into the water and rescues the drowning cub. The cute feline licks its savior all over; instantly bonding with the heroine.

Ibi carries the cub close to her chest, trying to keep the wet cat warm. She looks at the playful animal for a while, who itself is preoccupied with its frolicking with its rescuer. Ibi responds to the play of the cute cub by rubbing her own forehead on its; but her brief moment of delight is quickly lost for her worries about never seeing her mother again keeps recalling to her mind. Lost in her thoughts; Ibi stares into the waves of the river; then like a mirage, she sees the blurred wavy lettering, REJOICE in the water. Ibi also hears her name being called from behind, the image in the water fades away as she turns around, and to her surprise she sees her mother standing right before her.

The young lady's mother teases her excited daughter, "It has your inquisitive and stubborn nature, you know!"

Once more, Ibi's joy is quickly cut short, because she keeps remembering that her mother's visit is temporary. Ibi tell her mother that she still has one last trial to face but her mother reassures Ibi, saying, "That test has already been passed".

Ibi does not understand what her mother means, then it dons on her that her mother's ordeal at the point of giving birth to her, must be what her mother means by saying, "The test has already been passed".

Her mother triumphed over the enemy, by ensuring that the foretold Ẹdụlẹ́ is brought into this World safely.

Ibi's mom embraces her lonesome daughter, and gives Ibi the full account of their heritage; instructing the young warrior, about the gift and responsibility of the Ẹdụlẹ́.

The two ladies sit on the soft grass then the mother takes Ibi's hands in her own; as she reveals their history, "When the Celestial Guardians began to marry wives on Earth, the Black Leopard lord, protector of the forest and all things that grow took a wife from our tribe; her name was also Ibinabo, like yours; which means, a good thing has come. She bore the celestial angel a son who became a great king and ruled for many years, living longer than all men in his time. The Leopard lord blessed his wife's family with supernatural abilities because he was glad that his wife's family brought unexpected joy to him. The wife's younger sister got married and gave birth to a girl child, called, Adenbofa, meaning, no person is greater than you. She grew up strong and powerful and founded her own kingdom of protectors of the people. Her people called her Ẹdụlẹ́, the Black Panther. It was said that she had supernatural abilities and that a mysterious Black Panther fought beside her in battles and helped her defeat her powerful enemies. Since then one child born into the next generation of that family inherited the spirit of the Ẹdụlẹ́".

Ibi is speechless as her mother continues her tale, "So you see; every succeeding Ẹdụlẹ́ inherits the powers of all Ẹdụlẹ́s before her, giving each new hunter greater powers than the one before her or him.

So, when it is time, you will receive the accumulated gifts and strengths of my mother and our ancestors; and my powers too will pass on to you, making you a formidable warrior, possessing the speed and abilities of the Black Panther, the greatest hunter in the jungle; and your powers will give you the supernatural ability to track and defeat evil creatures that roam this World and many whose paths we have not yet crossed. Evil will hear your name and flee; you will fear no one, not even death".

Ibi sighs; her sad expression betrays her worries. Her mother smiles as she consoles her daughter, "I know your fear. It is the only fear we Ẹḍụḷẹ́s worry about but your fate will not be like mine. You will have a full life; bearing your own children and you will have that which I see in your eyes".

She raises Ibi's chin and giggles as she asks, "Tell me about him, what's his name? You can't hide it you know! True love reveals itself, it's written all over you; you have found someone, yes?"

Ibi doesn't say a word; she is too shy to talk about such things, especially being her first time. The mother prods her daughter deeper and tickles her all over. They both fall to their side and roll over, facing each other and staring into each other's eyes, Ibi answers her mother's question, "His name is Ade; we both came down here from England; actually unwillingly drafted into this mission. We never really talked much back home, even though we lived next to each other but something happened here in Ogoni; maybe being away from the many distractions back home has made us see things more clearly. We fell in love is all I can say; it all happened so fast, we both can't say how it did but as quickly as we found our love, so it is also that we have been separated".

Ibi pauses and looks at her mom, then ending her love story she concludes, "Our love was cut short, just like you and dad".

The mother cuddles her daughter as she tells her, "Losing a loved one shouldn't make us sad, it's never finding love that is really sad".

Ibi cries in her mother's arms; then wiping off Ibi's tears, her mother assures the young lover, "I promise you that your story will not end this way. I believe that after this is over and evil is vanquished, you and your Ade will have plenty of time to nurture your love".

The mom suddenly leaps up and reaches for a bunch of plants nearby. She plucks a purple flower from the bush and gives it to Ibi and request that her daughter gives it to her father when she gets back home in England; assuring the confused daughter; saying, "He'll understand; this flower was the symbol of our love for each other".

Ibi's mother embraces her daughter one last time and advises her that it will be dark soon; so the young traveler should be on her way. She walks her daughter to two huge trees and waves her hand across the space in between the trees. Suddenly a spiral wave of light appears between the two trees. She bids her daughter a final goodbye and tells her that she's happy to see her unborn child grown-up to become such a beautiful and strong woman. She counsels the young Seeker and gives her blessings, then standing there; she vanishes in front of Ibi.

The playful Leopard cub, which has been following Ibi all along, paws Ibi's foot and the Seeker carries the playful cub and walks through the pulsating portal.

Glimpse of a Dark Future

Meanwhile far away in his own dimension, Ade walks forward, stepping through a collapsed stone arch gateway, his eyes fixed on an abandoned crumbling building. "This doesn't look good", he mumbles as he looks around.

The apprehensive lad hesitates but treads slowly towards the spooky building; then a strange thought hits him; prompting him to halt his advance. He remembers the old Witch's curse then staggering backwards; as a cold shiver runs through his rigid body, he laments, "No, not again! Can it be? No, no, no, she wouldn't dare".

The terrified Seeker continues his cautious pace towards the entrance door, whispering as if talking to a partner, "What if that devil has actually opened the third gate of time; the door to the future? But this doesn't in anyway, look like the future, if anything it looks more like a decaying past".

Ade gets to the obscure front mesh door; his trembling hands carefully grab the rusty door handle. He gently turns the handle then suddenly swings the door open, hoping to scare away any rodents or reptiles.

Ade is confronted by a rock star looking zombie with a guitar strapped over his shoulder. Torn between waving a "Hi" and getting the hell out of there, the stunned hero remains motionless; and before Ade can gather his thoughts, the undead guitarist plucks his guitar string, sending an eerie note through the air and sending shivers through Ade's spine.

Ade quickly recollects himself; he dashes backwards as several undead match out towards him, chasing, crawling and reaching for the terrified Seeker. Soon Ade finds himself under attack by a horde of ravenous, drooling flesh-eaters.

The teaming host of the living-dead pours out from all around the premises almost catching up with Ade; running for his dear life, not looking forward, he rams into a rough textured frame. Ade is knocked to the ground, believing that he is done for, he shuts his eyes, expecting the first bite and afraid of turning to an undead himself. The loud roar of a huge dinosaur forces the goner to open his eyes, and standing tall above Ade are not the dreaded zombies but a Tyrannosaurus Rex.

Ade runs behind the giant animal, not at all considering the possibility of the gigantic brute devouring him. Ade's decision to align with the animal that he once helped, against the vicious Wormbeasts pays off.

The advancing multitude of zombies not intimidated by the size of the monstrous prehistoric animal, immediately focus their attack on the new intruder.

They swarm around the dinosaur, climbing, clawing and biting it all over but their tiny humanoid teeth do not penetrate the thick, scaly hide of the unshaken beast.

The Trex wastes no time in repelling the growling ghouls, he sidesteps from Ade and charges directly towards the pesky undead. The zombies are undeterred; soon they pile over the Trex like termites attacking an insect prey but the dinosaur is protected by its thick armoured skin.

In a counter move, the huge dinosaur swings its large tail from side to side, sweeping dozens of zombies off their feet. Continuing its counter move, it twists and shakes off all the mounted creatures from its body.

As the battle rages on, Ade picks up a stick and goes after the zombie guitarist, whose strings seem to be driving the undead attack. He attacks the zombie leader, hitting him all over. The undead guitarist falls to the ground and Ade raises his stick to crush the instrument when a high-pitched piercing scream rings behind Ade. Ade is temporarily dazed but shakes his head vigorously to recollect himself.

Ade turns around to find a gorgeously dress zombie Madame standing behind him. She stands calmly, wearing a red dress with an elaborately adorned vintage Sun hat and holding a bouquet of flowers, she begs Ade not to destroy the guitar. Ade is puzzled but raises his leg above the music instrument, ready to smash it. The undead woman introduces herself as the Czarina, empress of the undead realm. The zombies immediately stop their attack and stand still in the presence of their queen; the dinosaur also halts its aggression. Ade lowers his leg and walks nearer to the zombie queen. He notices that her body is completely formed of only bones; all flesh must have decayed over a long period; indicating that she must have existed as an undead for a very long time.

The Czarina apologises to Ade and the gentle giant for the initial misunderstanding. She explains that they were a community of peaceful farmers suddenly brought from the future to the present. She informs Ade that in the future a plague will sweep through the World, killing the entire population of humans and beasts. They do not know where the plague originated from but it started with strange a phenomenon in the sky followed by an invasion by foul beasts rising from the depths of the ground. Many people believed that it was the foretold apocalypse when the devil will rule over the Earth. She revealed further that soon after everyone perished in the World, the dead began to rise and not long after the World was inhabited by the undead.

Ade also introduces himself and explains his mission to recover a sacred weapon hidden by an ancient protector of mankind sent by the Creator Himself but the group of protectors deviated from their celestial duty and so lost the authority to carry on their obligation. Ade tells the undead queen that his journey led him through the triple gate of time and a Witch cast spells which opened the gates of the past as well as the future, thus merging three era into one; and now he must find a way to defeat the evil Witch and also find the weapon so that he can return on time to stop the apocalyptic invasion which is imminent.

The Czarina brings out a purple egg and hands it over to Ade, instructing him to place it in a pouch located at the back of the Witch. That will immobilize the evil witch and her curse trapping us all here will be broken and time will reset itself.

Ade doubts if he can get close to the powerful Witch, talk less of placing the egg in a pouch at her back, but he tells the undead queen that he must try.

The Czarina hands over the egg to Ade; and tells him, "Go now, do not fail, the future of all mankind is in your hands". She turns to Ade's loyal companion and charges the dinosaur, "Protect him".

Ade thanks the Czarina and walks away with his Dinosaur companion but the Czarina calls to him as he leaves. Ade turns around to hear what the zombie leader has to say. The Queen of the undead smiles and utters just one word, "REJOICE".

Ade bows to the undead queen and races after the dinosaur who leads the way back through the forest to Baba Yaga's jungle.

The Chasm of Dragons

The stone ring portal takes Alex away from the desolate land of the brown dragon into a majestic hall known as the Chasm of Dragons. The inside of the hall is decorated with aged marble walls and ceiling but it seems to have a bottomless Abyss, also known to many voyagers as the Gorge of Fire. The silence of the mansion sends cold shivers through the traveler's spine. He scans around, trying to decide where the exit lies. He sees another set of inscriptions on the glowing stone ring which reads, REJOICE; but Alex wonders what is there to rejoice about in an unfriendly bottomless hall which can only mean disaster. Alex notices that behind the set of ring portals is an open doorway and far beyond it, he sees a blue sky. The traveler decides to check out the only door when he is knocked over by a gust of whirlwind. When the air clears, he finds himself in the presence of a red dragon; this one much larger that the brown one, Alex knows that this is certainly the second dragon brother.

The dragon roars as he approaches the Seeker, bellowing with a thunderous howl, turning the quiet hall into a terrifying lair of death. Alex is petrified but remembers the advice of the rock head in the dark cave, so he summons the little courage he can muster and confronts the huge beast.

The adventurer greets his host, praising the monstrous creature but the angry dragon is nothing like his brown brother. This dragon is not taken into poetry or tales, he is a pure brute force of terror who abhors strangers; he doesn't make friends least of all, human friends.

Alex introduces himself to his new adversary, "Oh great dragon, mighty do you stand and great are your magnificent wings. I am a chosen adventurer, one of four; Seeker of the celestial weapon of old?"

The red dragon moves closer, showing himself clearer. He spreads his massive wings, clearly trying to intimidate the much smaller intruder. The colossal serpent answers his unmatched trespasser; speaking slowly, enunciating each word, he utters, "And why do you presume that I care about such things? I serve no master; neither do I fear any foe. My sole purpose is to lay waste any intruder who dares brave his way through my realm; but I see that you feign bravery even in the shadow of your imminent death".

The towering beast leans over Alex as he lies on the ground, intimidating the small human, "Now tell me; why will anyone send a lone Seeker into the belly of such a magnificent terror as me without a legion behind him?"

Alex stand to his feet, arms akimbo, showing more confidence; standing in defiance of the menacing dragon, "You are a being created by the Lord Creator himself and like all who dwell in the Universe, you must bow at the mention of His name. It is your duty to lend your support to my sacred mission and if not, you should step aside, lest you make yourself an enemy of God".

The angry red dragon ignores all what the brave traveler has said; instead he launches a vicious attack on the innocent traveler, aiming to crush him with his humongous foot".

Suddenly the huge red beast is knocked over by a great force. Getting up to his feet the red dragon is challenged by his own sibling, the brown dragon who has also been brought into the Chasm of Dragons by the stone ring portals.

Alex is caught between both dragon brothers, not sure which side he should run to but the advancing brown dragon walks past Alex straight to his large brother; snarling at his rival sibling, challenging his authority.

Racing past the brown dragon towards the red dragon, Alex tries to prevent a fight between two brothers; using his previous peace-maker calming technique he speaks to the wild dragon, "Look, we are not enemies and I am a man of peace. I'm sure we can be…"

The peacemaker's plea is cut short as the beastly dragon again tries to stomp on the insignificant human but the brown dragon pulls his new human friend out from under the trampling feet of his vicious brother.

The bigger dragon simmers down from his rage, then speaking with a sheepish smile, he mocks the human, "I can see you've already met my weak brother; as you can clearly see, he does not possess the grandeur and magnificence we serpents of old have. He should have been culled in the cradle or immediately he was born; showing up as a mere oversized bat, instead of a fierce dragonling, the terror our kind is known for. Pity he was spared in the nest, but here now, there's no one to save him or you from me".

Alex still unsure if any of the two dueling dragons is actually his friend, he asks the brown dragon, "Why do they do that? I mean, why do bullies always try to intimidate you by slurring their words?"

The older dragon comes closer to his smaller sibling and interrogates him, "Tell me, I'm curious; why you didn't eat him when you first encountered this human?"

As the two dragons carry on with their banter, Alex sneaks away towards the exit portal ring. He makes a quick run for the exit ring gate but his escape is dashed when he is cut off from the magical gate by the hostile red dragon.

The brown dragon nudges his big brother away from Alex; saving him from being trampled by the brother's large foot. Both dragons engage in a tail swiping fight but the brown dragon is no match for his violent sibling.

Both Alex and his new dragon friend try again to make a run for the final gate of time and space but they are cut off by the red dragon. Realising that his angry brother will kill his new friend, the brown dragon tells Alex, "We have to retreat".

A terrified Alex cries out loud; his voice drowned by the tumult of the two fighting dragons, "There is no-where to go!"

His protective dragon friend tells Alex to get on his back as he shouts, "We have to go back into the entry gate we came from!"

Alex climbs on to his friend's back however cautions his winged friend against his escape plan, reminding his winged steed that going back into an already exited ring portal will be disastrous but the already airborne beast ignores the warning and flies straight into the collapsing ring gate. The two companions cry out as they plunge into the unstable portal, their voices fading away as they disappear.

They find themselves lost in a void, floating between realms, passing through several morphing portals. The pair continues their voyage together; the man riding his friendly dragon, flying high up searching for a passage out of the uncharted World. Alex remembers the last inscriptions etched on the entry ring-gate. He then recites the word over and again, "Rejoice, rejoice, rejoice…"

As Alex's chant continues, his travelling companion shouts out in excitement, "Look!"

Alex stops his chants and concurs, "Yes, I see it. I see the bright light".

They fly straight into the vortex of bright light; just like the one that carried Alex and his three fellow Seekers through the Universe.

Alex steps into the portal then looks behind him to make sure his new friend is tagging along but the brown dragon sits still. Alex is moved to tears; he runs back to the dragon and tries to force him up but the brown dragon is adamant telling his human pal, "I know my red brother is incorrigible but he is all alone there, in that scorched World and he is family, so I can't leave him there by himself. I have to find my way back and look for him. Don't worry, he'll only get mad, he won't hurt me".

With that, Alex decides to proceed with his appointed task. He walks through the portal, turning back, pausing now and again, waving to his gentle beast buddy".

A Hero Forged by Fire

Makato extends his arm towards the heavenly weapon, reaching out to the Blazing Sword as if to feel it, to be sure it is truly real but the patience of the lynching gang is over stretched. With no one to halt the murderous pack, the fate of the Seeker is sealed.

Fate however, seems to be on Makato's side again, for the traveler is saved for the second time; this time by a flash of light beaming upon the multitude; causing the entire fierce creatures to shield themselves and cowering in trepidation at the sight of the arriving terror.

The blinding light dims revealing a four winged being. A Cherub announces his presence by chanting, "REJOICE, REJOICE, REJOICE!".

This Cherub is a high ranking heavenly guard placed outside the boundary of the earthly paradise by the Creator to prevent any mortal from entering the tabooed garden after its inhabitants were cast out. Neither man nor beast, the Cherub has four faces yet presents only a single appearance to those who look upon it. Humans perceive and relate to a human face; wild animals see only the Lion face; domestic animals communicate with an Ox face, while birds of the sky perceive and speak to its Eagle face. For a fierce guard that it is, its four majestic white wings do not translate its ferocious nature. One pair droops down like weapons secured at a warrior's side while the other pair flaps gently at its back sometimes lifting the ten foot being; hovering it a few inches above the ground, and also ready to lift the agile defender in an instant. At the end of each wing is a hand with five digits, like that of a man, gesticulating as it speaks.

The Cherub is the guard charged with the responsibility to prevent any mortal from entering the forbidden garden and given the authority to maintain order in the bordering forest.

The angel rebukes the wild beasts, speaking to them with an imposing tone, informing them that indeed there was a prophesy of a stranger coming to the forest but it was foretold that the outsider would come to free them from their bondage in the forbidden forest, so that one day they can be integrated into the larger World populated by mankind, and eventually find their place amongst other beasts and animals on Earth.

The angel lifts up the badly bruised man then embraces him, wrapping the injured traveler with its wings. Suddenly the wings start to glow and Makato's wounds begin to heal. Like a miracle, Makato fully recovers; his bruises disappear and his strength returns; even his stained and torn clothes are restored as if nothing had happened to them.

The Cherub tells Makato the story of the inhabitants of the garden who were tasked with the singular duty to tend the garden and care for the animals but they disobeyed the Creator and so were chased out of the sacred garden, then a blazing sword was placed outside the garden, encircling the perimeter; turning in all directions, sizzling in a continuous flame, preventing all mortals from entering the garden.

The Cherub also narrates the sad ending to the Seeker, telling him how the humans moved away, to look for a new home, leaving the other expelled beasts unnamed; for it was the man's duty to name every beast in the garden. Those who got named migrated to distant lands, forming new herds but those who never got a name became confused, without an identity; they did not know where they belonged. Considering themselves as outcasts, their minds brewed with anger and they formed a world here and created a population of outcasts outside the garden, in this forest; clinging to one another, slaying any stranger who strays into their forest.

Filled with pity, the virtuous Seeker walks amongst the still growling beasts and calls each one according to their shape or face and some according to their temperament. The descendant of the cast out human ancestors gives names to the savaged beasts. One by one, the animals and beings begin to simmer down as they get an identity, their anger quenched as they are called by a name, given by the foretold hero that will one day come.

Then the Cherub stretches his long arm and seizes the blazing sword, immediately extinguishing the encircling fire and clearing and opening a clear entrance into the garden of old. Not wasting any time, the celestial giant leads Makato through the magnificent archway into the legendary garden.

CHAPTER 14: PARAGONS OF VIRTUE

Unconditional Love

Ibi emerges on the other side of the blue ring portal; cuddling the Leopard cub. Standing before her are four unusual beings from the Feline Tribe. They have human form but their heads are catlike. Their skin is patterned like that of a Leopard. Ibi knows immediately that she has found the lost tribe of the Ẹdụlẹ́ descendants. Their skin is golden yellow, with a smooth light fur, it has a uniform pattern of black spots and golden rosettes across their entire body, resembling cat paws; indicative of the genealogy of the feline lineage.

The stone walls of the aged building are intricately decorated with markings representing major events in their evolution. The architecture can easily pass for that of the Aztec civilization. There are rows of pillars on all four sides of the large courtyard where Ibi stands; which itself is surrounded by a passageway. Stout guards of the same tribe stand still on two levels of the broad structure. The temple-like building is planted in the middle of a dense forest, one extending as far as the eyes can see. No animals are seen around the courtyard but it is clear that this tribe is the dominant species in this kingdom.

The four cat women remain in their demure stance, then stretching their arms; they indicate a welcoming gesture and then lead the way towards a wide steep flight of steps. They stop at the bottom of the stairway but indicate that their visitor should proceed upwards. Ibi picks up the little cub which she had dropped to play around. Ibi can hear the sounds of birds far away in the forest but none can be seen around; not surprising, for any self respecting bird will surely keep its distance from a large family of cat-people.

She carries the cute squeaking little rascal and gently takes one step after another, leaving a gathering of catlike women staring at her from below. At the top of the building, Ibi meets the leader of the tribe, simply called Father, he leads the ancient tribe alongside his wife, who also is simply called Mother. Protecting the ruling couple are two muscular male guards. The leader welcomes Ibi, reciting a praise which the elated visitor doesn't understand. Ibi shows respect to the royals by curtsying. They reply to their guest in English, welcoming her in a more familiar way. A Black Panther strolls into their midst, closely followed by a Leopard. The little cub struggles to get down to get to the two massive cats; who are themselves busy sniffing the stranger. It is clear to Ibi that the cub is the child of the Leopard pair.

She drops the eager cub gently and watches as it hops on its Black Panther father, while the Leopard mother licks her little cub all over.

The leader of the tribe breaks Ibi's short distraction and tells her, "You have your mother's eyes".

Ibi has heard that before; once form the Oracle back at Ogoni and hearing it now does not come as a surprise to her. She replies the elderly leader, "Yes, so I have been told".

Ibi tries to explain to the leader that she found the cub straying in the forest and wading in the river, beyond their domain on the other side of the portal, probably drowning; but the leader simply nods and introduces the Seeker to his wife. The tribe's Mother greets Ibi and tells her that the little cub knows that it is watched over at all times and was never really in any danger. She then pledges to the bold Seeker that so it will be for her also from now on; she'll be protected by the entire clan at all times; and whenever danger lurks, help will come to her wherever she maybe.

The leader then tells Ibi, "Your mother was a powerful Ẹdụlẹ́, and I can see in your eyes, her fire. We will invoke the spirit of the Ẹdụlẹ́ and it will feel your spirit and decide if both your spirit and his are in agreement".

Continuing; he tells the young Seeker, "Your mother stopped a great evil from entering our World and so prevented a great calamity from befalling us all; for that we are eternally grateful for her supreme sacrifice. Her unconditional love has paid for your final test and so you are exempted from any further test. You will be taken straight to the den of the Ẹdụlẹ where you will receive the spirit of the Ẹdụlẹ. You will feel the strength of the greatest hunter in the jungle; the Black Panther".

The leader sees in Ibi, the expression of curiosity; so he tells the unsettled guest, "One does not need to be a mind reader to see in your eyes that something puzzles you".

The young lady answers, "Yes, if I may be bold to ask; how did you and your tribe come to be here; I mean, where do you come from?"

The father of the cat people recalls the long struggle of his people; as he narrates to Ibi, "It all started when the Watcher angels began to choose wives from amongst the people of the World. Ẹdụlẹ, the Guardian angel responsible for caring for the land and all things that grow, chose a beautiful strong-willed woman among two sisters, from your tribe. She later bore him a child who took the father's form and powers. The other sister, who also was known to be a warrior and defender of her people became lonely for her only sister was with her new husband; so the Ẹdụlẹ angel gifted his powers to the sister of his wife so that she can also fulfill her destiny as the protector of her people. She became the first Ẹdụlẹ. Sometime later, the people's warrior also got married and begat a daughter. It was then discovered that the mother's powers passed on to her child, making her the second Ẹdụlẹ, protector of the people. Over time the role of the Ẹdụlẹ became more than just protecting the people against mortal enemies, for an evil descended upon the World, so Ẹdụlẹ assumed a greater responsibility; one that will make her the protector of all people both in her village and beyond her land, covering the entire World. The child of the first sister; wife of the Guardian angel; passed the gene of their catlike father to her descendants and they too passed their form to their descendants and that was how the Feline tribe has expanded and thrived. Over the years, mankind began to treat our kind as outcast and our way of life became increasingly unacceptable to humans. So our ancestors migrated for many generations until finally they established this kingdom, far away and hidden from the World of men".

The leader also tells Ibi that the Watcher angel, Ẹdụlẹ́ and his fellow Guardian angels fell out of God's favour for their sin of procreating with humans and teaching Mankind various crafts which brought strife and destruction to the World. After the flood which God caused to cleanse the World, many of the Guardians perished but nine Guardian angels, including Ẹdụlẹ́ were spared in the flood. The nine surviving angels knew that without the favour of the Almighty, they would not have the grace to defeat the enemy, so they hid their celestial weapons with various tribes whom they considered worthy. Our progenitor, kept his weapon with us, hidden from the World and the enemy until a hero, proves worthy of its powers".

The Leader of the cat tribe also warns the seeker, "I don't know what evil awaits you back in the World but I know it will be a lot stronger than that which took your mother's life".

The leader again reminds Ibi that though she will not face any further ordeal, she must still enter the old sealed cave where the weapon of the guardian is laid. He tells the anxious Seeker that there can only be one Ẹdụlẹ́ in the World at any time; and the spirit of the Ẹdụlẹ́ guardian angel will be upon her inside the den and she must endure the immense power to become the new Ẹdụlẹ́ warrior and protector; if she falters, she will be consumed by the energy and will die. Ibi is taken by the Mother of the tribe and led to the cave.

Ibi is given one last advice by the leader, "The power of an Ẹdụlẹ́ must be executed justly and with reservation at all times for with great power comes great responsibility".

The seal of the cave is broken and Ibi walks into the dark den unaccompanied. Outside the cave the feline tribesmen and women sing and chant praises then they hear the thunderous sound raging from inside the cave, until suddenly it all goes quiet and then a loud roar is heard followed by a cloud of dust. When it all clears, Ibi matches out slowly but boldly; she's been transformed. Her hair is changed to a wild mane of dreadlocks; her eyes peering with a red glow, her earthly clothes changed into a warrior's garb; even her strides, though strong, are as silent as that of a prowling hunting Leopard. She is the new Ẹdụlẹ́; treading by her right side is a huge Black Panther and on her left is a fierce golden Leopard. The entire feline colony shouts, "Ẹdụlẹ́, Ẹdụlẹ́!" The leader of the feline tribe nods in reverence and his wife courtesy to receive the new protector of mankind.

Hope Rekindled

Ade gets to Baba Yaga's forest but his dinosaur companion is not there; he finds the Witch's house standing at the same spot he last saw it. Ade knows that the old Witch cannot be far away as he stares at the spooky house, swaying, and occasionally twitching like a grasshopper in a termite's nest.

Ade runs in circles as he searches around the tall trees in the cold misty jungle but neither the Trex nor Baba Yaga are there. Ade walks back to the triple gates treading carefully, looking out for the old Witch.

Suddenly the old Witch drops silently from the hidden bushy crown of a tall tree and lands on the Seeker, crushing him to the ground. She rants in her screeching voice, "I've got you now, foolish boy; you think you can escape me; none has escaped the entrapment of my triple time spell".

Sitting over the knocked down traveler, Baba Yaga raises her crooked staff above Ade's head and slams down the Witching stick; laughing, boasting in a croaky voice, "If I can't lick your tongue, then I will chew your tongue. Now, bite the dust!"

But instead of the stick smashing on her victim's head, it locks firmly in the huge jaws of Ade's prehistoric defender".

The Trex swings the old Witch and her staff away from his fallen friend. Ade springs to his feet and confronts the old hag, ordering her, "I'm not afraid of you and I will never kiss your rotten mouth; now release me, undo the time spell!"

Baba Yaga squawks and shrills loudly; creeping on all fours; twisting and contouring like a worm burning in brine; as she approaches her challenger. The Trex stomps between Baba Yaga and Ade, shielding the brave young man.

Baba Yaga crawls backwards trembling with fear as the huge dinosaur matches ferociously towards her. She pleads with the advancing animal, appealing desperately but cunningly, "Oh, mighty lizard king, ruler of the ancient era, spare me this prey, so I can feast on his luscious tongue and I will grant you easy passage back to your domain".

Ignoring the Witch's trickery, the giant dinosaur tramples on her, crushing her bony body on the dry hard ground but Ade yells out quickly to his strong protector; persuading him that they need her alive.

The dinosaur flips the defeated Witch over, exposing the socket in her back; which the zombie queen spoke about. Immediately, Ade places the purple egg in the dent compelling the Witch to become subservient to the Seeker. Baba Yaga stands up, still under the influence of the mystical egg, then waving her magic staff; she reverses the three gates of time.

A gust of wind immediately starts to form within each of the three gates, then like a suction pump, each gate begins to suck back all which it had expelled. The zombie horde gets pulled into the gate of the future; at the same time, the gate of the past pulls-in the noble dinosaur as it closes.

The dinosaur begins to fade as it is being swallowed back from whence it came. Ade runs to his prehistoric friend. Ade is emotional as he hugs the huge animal and tries to hold on to the Trex as it is being sucked into the closing time portal.

The dinosaur also moans as he is finally separated from his human friend. Ade walks into the middle gate; he fades into the large time gate sending him to a different era; aligning the traveler to his initial set path.

Ade is transported to the land of his ancestors; to the World beyond our World; the dominion of the keepers of the staff of Kings. Ade is received by the high priest; who cleanses the Seeker to free him of any unclean spirits and thoughts. Ade is then led up the steep stairs by two maidens to the sacred shrine.

The keeper of the shrine welcomes the Seeker, announcing to all, "Hope for mankind is rekindled!"

The Strength of Faith

Alex walks through the portal into a surreal World. He notices that there are dragons there as well, resting peacefully on the marble floor; but these dragons are not like the aggressive serpents he encountered; they seem domesticated, more like the canine companions of his World.

The Seeker is received by a maiden who immediately walks the traveler to their leader, the Faerie Queen of the Dragon Realm.

There are strong armed male guards fully clad in warring armour posted to strategic posts. Also gathering around the queen, attending to the leader are several female and male court advisers. She introduces herself to the stranger, "I am Athena, Faerie Queen of the Dragon Kingdom, welcome to our World".

Alex pauses for a moment then asks, "Faeries? I thought those were just mythical beings only found in folklore and children stories".

The Faerie Queen responds to Alex, "Well, maybe some of those children tales are real after all, taken from real life experiences of voyagers".

The Faerie Queen speaks a strange language to her court aides but English to Alex. She explains to Alex that the Faerie people of the Dragon kingdom have the gift of speaking in various tongues and she the Queen can pick up indications from others when there is an unsettling thought in their mind.

She asks the visitor, "I will like to know how you managed to pass through the realm of the dragon brothers. They were cast out of this kingdom many centuries ago, when the older and more impatient red brother led his milder sibling to rebel against our ways and attack our people".

Alex shakes his head and recounts to the beautiful Faerie Queen, "Frankly, I didn't do anything. I only knew that I didn't possess the strength to fight either of them, so I tried to talk them out of a fight. When that didn't work for the brown dragon, I had to create a distraction and run away. Later, when I was confronted by the fierce red brother, the brown dragon saved me; I'm not sure why, but I guess he wasn't that bad a dragon after all; he probably just needed a pal".

The Queen enlightens the traveler that dragons are creatures of immense strength and sometimes supernatural abilities, yet for all their powers, they are very distrusting of all who they meet for the first time. She explains to Alex that because of their suspicious nature, they often find themselves living alone, far from intruders but that itself creates a loneliness which soon turns to aggression. So the ancient serpents are their own undoing; isolating themselves even though they are meant to be social beings. She tells her visitor that they have since nurtured a new generation of dragons in the kingdom to be part of the community and many of the magnificent beasts have been adopted into people's homes, living with families as companions or pets.

The Faerie Queen tells the inquisitive lad where she and her people came from and how they came to live in the hidden realm. She tells Alex, "Our people once lived amongst the humans of your known World for a very long time until humans became aware of the abilities of faeries to grant fortunes and confer powers to whomever they wished. Over time, the greed of men began to fester and they hunted and captured many of our kind. Our people were not authorized to destroy humans, so they decided to leave your World to make a new life for themselves".

She reveals further, "The most powerful faeries, who had lived for thousands of years put their powers together and transformed our land into an unseen World, hidden in time and dimension, leaving only a few stone Ring-Portals open only to a chosen few to pass through".

Alex queries the leader, "I've been meaning to ask; was that you in the cave of the rock head? I heard a voice in my head and it sounded just like you now".

The Faerie Queen smiles as she replies to the bemused traveler, "Yes, it was I. I did not doubt you for one moment".

Still inquisitive, Alex asks further, "Doubt about what?"

The Faerie Queen smiles again as she answers the still puzzled young man, "That you can find your way here; yes, there were trials along the way and even there was the chain of self doubt, but sometimes all we need is someone to believe in us, to get us to start believing in ourselves".

She walks ahead as she invites Alex to her kingdom, "We are glad and honoured to have you here".

Alex is not done with his questions, he inquires, "Here? Where is this place exactly; I know you have said that your ancestors hid your new home in an unseen space but are you still within our Earth?"

The Queen replies, "This realm is uncharted; hidden in time and space within the vast Universe, far away from your World. It is the new land of the Faeries protected from humans and other hostile creatures that roam the vast Universe. Many have journeyed through space and time, searching for various lost objects of old and their paths have sometimes led them to our kingdom. We are the keepers of things and knowledge that must not be lost, yet be kept secret until the right time comes for it to be revealed".

Alex still wanting to know more about the mysterious place, asks, "Are we in the present era or the past?" The Queen leading the way and followed by her court aides; replies, "Here time has many dimensions, you are in your time and we exist in ours".

Alex, not giving up on his interrogation, quickens his steps to catch up with his host, imploring her, "I don't understand!"

The Faerie leader stops walking and turns to her youthful guest and nods as she answers, "I know! Now come with me; the Elder's Council awaits you. They have expected the chosen one for many ages. The elders will wish to know you before they entertain any of your streams of questions".

The Queen Faerie and Alex walk into a cluster of stone domes set close to one another, with rough stone walkways connecting the houses. Understandably, there are no vehicles of any kind; the people move about on tamed dragons. There are no trees or grasses but several potted plants can be seen dotted at entrances of important buildings. Stone statues of their ancestors adorn the hard landscape. The air is scented with a mild lavender smell and there is no noise but a chime-like resonance of continuous gentle ringing in the air. Standing in the middle of a large square is a huge building, decorated with symbolic engravings and writings in unfamiliar text. In all, the kingdom looks and feels like a place of great wealth.

At the Council hall the Faerie Queen presents Alex to the administrator of the Council; who welcomes the stranger and immediately announces his arrival to the Council. Alex quickly realises that the women are revered more and are mostly ranked higher than the men; who strangely age much faster than the women.

It seems like the process of child bearing secretes a hormone which rejuvenates the anatomy of the women and prepares them for another reproductive cycle; for the gestation period of their unborn child is equivalent to three human years.

The regal chamber is packed full of richly dressed men and women, eager to catch a glimpse of the chosen hero of men. The women's clothing looks similar to that of the Queen; light, flowing silk dresses with delicate silver filigree trimmings while the men, looking much older than their female counterparts and having long beards; are dressed in white ancient Greek-like cloaks fastened at the shoulders with a brooch.

Alex bows nervously to the esteemed men and women, who are seated in hierarchical groups in the great chamber.

The Faerie Queen sits at the head of the Council, listening but not interrupting the elders as they grill the unknown traveler one by one and the Seeker patiently answering all their questions.

After the Council is satisfied, they explain to the confirmed hero that they have expected him for ages since the Watcher angel; the Falcon angel, Heru brought his celestial force, Mana; to them for safe keeping and preservation.

The Faerie Queen congratulates the seeker, telling him, "Though you were filled with self doubt, you endured through the ordeals and finally your faith in those who chose you for this task has seen you through to the end of your trials".

Then she hands over Alex to the high priest to begin the transfer rites of the celestial force to the chosen one.

The Value of Sacrifice

Far away in another World, the Cherub leads Makato into the hallowed garden. The Seeker is overwhelmed by the magnificence of the sacred land. He is filled with tears for the excitement is too intense for the traveler. The garden is a vast land comprising of mountains and rivers; more of a small country than what Makato envisaged. The Cherub and the traveler stand for a while appreciating the size and splendor of the massive land and the tranquility of the uninhabited country. Still in awe, Makato asks his host, "I don't think anyone in the World would have imagined how big this place is. If this vast land is considered just a mere garden planted especially for man, I can't imagine what the domain of the Almighty will be like".

The Cherub beckons to the dumbfounded Seeker, "Come, let us go in, there is much to see and a lot to talk about".

The Cherub carries the Seeker and flies across the silvery river and over the water falls cascading from the mountains. Makato is astonished by the splendour of the landscape.

Finally the Celestial guide lands in the middle of an ornate garden. As if he can tell, Makato asks, "Why, in the middle of such a flowery garden is a dead tree still standing?" The Cherub remains silent and Makato continues his interrogation, "No, no, no, don't tell me that this is the tree… the tree that bore the fruit, the Tree of Knowledge!"

The emotionless Cherub replies, "Indeed it is. It was this tree that bore an abundance of diverse fruits; each fruit bestows a different gift of knowledge from the others; so that any human who consumes it would gain immense knowledge; but remember that knowledge is not the same as wisdom; for knowledge without wisdom create nothing more than clever devils".

The Cherub warns further, "Like all gifts, the fruits of this tree also had its taboos".

Makato walks around the dead tree, gazing up and down its dried bark as the Cherub explains more, "It was the serpent, possessed by the fallen one, who plucked the first fruit. Though he could not partake of it, he offered it to the woman who lived here, who in turn offered it to her mate. Though the tree was planted for their own future consumption, the immature humans were not ready to receive the seductive powers of knowledge. Their eyes became open but they could not see what damage they had caused. To protect them from themselves, the Almighty barred them from the garden, lest they consume more of the revealing fruits".

Makato out of curiosity asks, "So why is the tree still standing, will it bloom again or is it to serve as a reminder of the betrayal of man?"

The Cherub replies, "No one can uproot or cut down the tree, though dead; because it was planted by the Creator Himself and it is only He who can decide the fate of the tree of promise".

The Seeker looks downcast, arms crossed on chest and his head dropping down, Makato is lost in his own thoughts. The Celestial guide breaks the Seeker's pensive mood, telling him, "I know what you are thinking and what your next question will be".

He leads the Seeker to another location in the garden, filled with various scented flowering plants, the Cherub points at a vacant spot, "There, that was its place; the holy spot where the Tree of Life was planted". Makato is filled with a deep sense of sorrow but suddenly, the flowers rearrange themselves, forming the word, "REJOICE".

The Cherub reveals the hidden to the Seeker; pointing to the middle of the bunch of flowers, "The tree of Life once took root here but the Creator removed it, for there was no more need of it here. It was created for the Creator's favourite children, and since they lived here no more, The Almighty took the blooming tree away".

The Cherub counsels Makato; explaining to the Seeker; that since he, the awaited hero has come, the sacred garden will wither; for the almighty has given man the opportunity to create many gardens, which He has promised to visit and mingle with his most precious creation, His human children. When two or more people are gathered in his name, represented by the sacred flame of pure love; the Father will be drawn to their presence.

Makato is confused, he turns to his guide and queries the erudite giant, "Well, I know we are in an extraordinary garden but that was a bit unexpected; what does that mean?"

The emotionless Cherub explains the flower transformation to the puzzled mortal, "Indeed, you are the chosen one to come here and the garden is speaking to you. It wants you to be of good hope".

The Cherub further reveals to the human that in the beginning of our consciousness, the Almighty set out to create a new World and so He ordered his angels; giving them the authority to make real what He already created within Himself. After all creation was complete, the Almighty, who in His glory is too great to fellowship with the lesser Celestials; needed a new being to have communion with; for we that existed around Him could not venture close, for His essence is too great and will instantly consume us, so He decided to make a new being; one that will be a resemblance of Him and who will possess part of His essence; so that the new creation will be able to withstand the intense glory whenever the Creator comes near. So man and woman were made and spread around the World. Amongst the pairs created, one was most pleasing to the Almighty. So He planted this garden for them and the Almighty visited them often in this garden; but when the man and his mate were chased out and they lost the favour of the Father, there was no one left in the garden for the Almighty to fellowship with; but because the Father so loved his children and wished for them to be redeemed, He set a course in motion. After many ages passed, one man showed the godliness in his heart and the Father considered him just and obedient. So as a final test, the Father ordered the old man to offer his only child as Sacrifice to Him, his God. The just man did not hesitate but the Almighty intervened before the child was harmed; for the Almighty saw in the man's heart how much he loved and revered Him. So, the Creator found mankind worthy again to be redeemed. He then offered His own son to be a sacrifice for the World for even as omnipotent as He is, He obeys His own laws, lest He be accused by the self-proclaimed accuser; of overlooking the transgression of his disobedient children. Now that the penalty for man's sin has been borne, the severed relationship between the Father and His children has been restored. So the Father has granted that where any two or more of His children are gathered in the eternal flame of love, He will be drawn to their presence and at that place and moment an Eden will exist.

The Cherub takes Makato back to the edge of Eden and they both walked out of the sacred garden, sealing it forever. Then the Cherub enclasps the chosen one in an embrace with its wings, conferring its powers to the new hero of man. He then orders Makato to stretch out his hand; and the weapon that guarded the garden for ages slowly drifts to the Samurai's hand. Makato raises the Blazing sword as he proclaims loudly, "I rejoice in the Lord, for hope is rekindled".

Immediately all the beasts and beings of the forbidden forest bow to the chose one.

PART FOUR:

THE WAR OF
THE GODS

CHAPTER 15: HEROES REBORN

Only three returns

Ibi, Alex and Makato emerge from the same gates they each set out from, but Ade has not come through his gate. As the new heroes of men step out, they are received by their individual mentors; the Oracle welcomes Ibi, calling the reborn Seeker by her new name, Ẹdụlẹ́. Alex is received by Chief Kabaka while the war deity, Egbesu acknowledges the arrival of Makato the Samurai. Sàngó stands alone as he awaits his protégé but Ade does not come forth.

Chief Kabaka laments, "They have come back the same; without the Heavenly weapons; and Ade has not returned. We are doomed, we have lost our leading warrior and the fourth weapon; hope is lost".

Ibi turns to Chief Kabaka; her eyes are troubled by the thought of losing her love, but her gaze is drawn away to the old Priestess, who seeing the worry in Ibi's eyes, disagrees with the Chief, "No! We should rejoice; we have three champions and three weapons; they have accomplished their sacred tasks. Do not ask them what they have seen but trust that they have received the power of the Watchers". She adds, pointing to Ade's gate, "Look, his gate is still standing. That means he is still alive and there is still hope of his return; we have to give him time".

Egbesu cuts in, "Quiet everyone! Look up, there are no birds flying; no crickets chirping, the air is cold and the clouds are fading. Death is coming".

Sàngó calls for action, "We can no longer wait for Ade, time is not on our side, we have to find their source and destroy it, I believe Ade hasn't completed his quest, so he will not be released to us yet; we must leave now!"

The Oracle charges Ibi, "I feel the hunter's spirit within you; you are the Ẹdụlẹ; you can find the enemy's location, even as it is veiled from our own eyes; you possess the ability to find them; hunt them!"

Ibi sniffs the air around her, like a predator scenting for her prey, then she snarls, bearing her teeth like a prowling big cat then runs ahead through the clearing which surrounds the stone circle and heads into the woods; the others follow her.

The group wastes no time, they follow the human hunter, racing behind Ibi's as she creates a new track through the bushes. Soon the company of warriors finds itself in an endurance race as they try to keep up with Ibi and her superhuman strength.

The group of seven runs for miles through woods and fields, through entangling vines and soggy swamps until the strain begins to tell on the old Oracle; then like once before; this time, Sàngó picks up the tiring old Priestess on his broad arm and the sprint continues.

After racing for several miles, Chief Kabaka halts the trail, gasping, trying to catch his breath.

Egbesu walks up to the big man and asks sarcastically, "Don't tell me you want me to carry you or do you?"

Chief Kabaka ignores Egbesu for his concerns seem more that that of fatigue; he asks the Oracle, "It just occurred to me that we don't have any attack or defense plan nor a retreat strategy; what do we do after we find them? What if their strength or number is too great for us to defeat?"

Alex lends his voice, "Yes, I've wondered about that myself, how can we defeat something that cannot die?" Sàngó is not bothered about that, he urges, "Let us find them first, then we can decide how to destroy them".

The wise old Priestess assures the troubled chief, "You of all people should know that it has not been by our power that we have endured this fight for so long, battling these creatures of old has only been made possible by our faith that good triumphs over evil and the hope that one day, they will be vanquished".

The tracker then resumes her search for the location of the Ogoni beacon; where the enemies might be gathering.

At the Edge of War

The tracker warrior suddenly stops her hunt and the group halts their run, they remain quiet, slowly closing up to Ibi then the Oracle asks the female warrior, "What do you perceive?"

Ibi snaps out of her hunting mode, as if breaking from a spell; then pointing from within the woods at a large clearing far ahead; Ibi tells her companions, "They are over there".

Alex stares into the distance but like the others, he cannot see what Ibi's extrasensory perception enables her to clearly see.

Sàngó gazes deeply at the identified location but even his big eyes perceive nothing. The fire giant turns at their guide for any further observation but Ibi, still shadowing the invisible enemy is too engrossed to be distracted. Sàngó shakes Ibi out of her engrossed stalking watch then asks her, "What do you see?"

With her gaze still fixed on the unseen enemy as if monitoring every move of theirs, Ibi describes what she sees, "There are two huge devices, one on that hill, the other at the foot of the hill; I think these two are the beacons we are looking for; but the entire area is sprawling with vile looking creatures. These are not earthly beings for sure. I think I can identify the leader; from your previous descriptions, I believe it is Demonicus itself. Its thick hide and enormous wings are flaming red and it has two large horns sticking out from its forehead and curves all the way back, like a ram's horn".

Egbesu and Sàngó both sigh at the same time and Sàngó confirms their worst fears, "That's him alright, that is Brutus Demonicus, hell's champion on earth; Egbesu and I fought him once; we were no match for him, and I'm afraid we don't stand a chance with him even now; he is unstoppable".

Before Sàngó can catch his breath, Ibi reveals more, "Well, if you couldn't defeat him then, I'm sorry to tell you that this time he is not alone. It seems he has brought a whole army of demons, a hundred at least, and it seems the ground is spitting out more of them".

Egbesu shouts aloud, "They're coming from the ground?"

Sàngó hushes his mate, "Be quiet, if they hear us, we will be doomed for sure".

Makato; who has been silent all this while squeezes through the crowding allies and gently taps Ibi on her shoulder, and tells her to take her time to tell them all what she sees.

Ibi stares into the oblivion for a moment, then continues calmly, "On the hill with the Brutus is a black wolf; it's bigger than any canine I've ever seen. I think it's the one the Seer told us about, back at the Monastery; it is the master's pet, never leaving his side. The beacon on the hill must be the main transmitter; it must be why Brutus himself is guarding it. At the base of the hill is a Taurus creature watching over a huge devil-horn beacon and standing with the part man, part bull beast is a terrifying Manticore; a beast once thought to exist only in fairy-tale stories; it has the head of a demon, the body of a lion, the tail of a scorpion and wings made of a stretched skin membrane. Down below are several faceless tall humanoids, with tentacles protruding from their backs. One of these creatures stabbed Alex in London, when we encountered them; Sàngó saved Alex's life. I can see all around the open field, the ground seems to be opening up like sores and things are coming out, both mighty and small; they are too diverse and too many to describe or count".

Makato stops the clairvoyant warrior, bowing like a Samurai that he is and thanking her for the useful information.

The Ninja warrior then asks his comrades, "Now that we know what we are up against, what do we do?"

Egbesu quickly cautions the group, telling them that they must act discreetly and not alert their enemy until the group agrees on an attack strategy.

Alex shakes his head, telling the undecided group, "Don't look at me; I'm new to demons and foul beasts. Just sound the attack bell and you'll have my force".

Egbesu appeals to Sàngó again, "We need him, put away your petty quarrel; just call him; both of you are like twins, you alone can sense where he is right now and so only you can call upon him".

Sàngó interrupts the war deity and refuses his request.

Alex supports Egbesu's call, insisting that if Sàngó knows anyone who can bolster their force, Sàngó should definitely summon him. When the thunder deity refuses to budge, Alex asks, "It's that guy who beat you to get the girl, isn't it?"

Alex's teasing draws Sàngó's ire, igniting his short temper but the Oracle quickly controls the escalating tension and suggests that they close in on the location then Ibi can pronounce the order; telling the invaders that they must disband, and hopefully that will make the devils realise that their cover is blown and so they'll cease their cloaking spell. Suddenly they hear a rustling sound in the bushes behind; which instantly triggers the two giants to take a defense formation, ready for battle. As the cracking sound of breaking twigs draws closer, the team becomes tense; but the tension is relaxed when they see a familiar face.

Ibi's is the first to spring forward, knocking the new comer to the ground; it's Ade, the fourth Seeker.

The excited friends are happy to see the delayed hero. The four warriors bond together, hugging and frisking one another, like a mother checking for bruises on her child.

The Oracle heaves a sigh of relief and rejoices aloud, "May the Almighty be praised, our strength has soared".

Alex tells his returned friend, "You are a sight for sour eyes; you kept us worrying all day".

Ibi holding on to Ade gives the new comer a quick update and asks if he agrees with their attack strategy.

Ade's response is brief; taking command of the company, he orders, "We go to war now!"

As the group of Earth defenders march out of the woods towards the mountain and hill which they know is teaming with the hidden army from hell, the four human-warriors step ahead one by one proclaiming the virtue they offer.

Ade announces to the group as he boldly marches closer to the shrouded battle ground, "I bring us HOPE of victory this day".

Ibinabo follows closely, affirming, "I bring us the strength of a bonding LOVE".

Next is Alex who states, I bring us the FAITH that all is well".

Makato completes the solemn oaths as he affirms, "I bring us the reward of a selfless SACRIFICE".

The Transformation

Ade addresses his comrades, "Well, finally the wait is over, now we are here, at the edge of the battle of all battles, the war of all wars".

Şàngó and Egbesu stand at the back of the Oracle and Chief Kabaka; then the four Seekers begin to transform into their newly acquired status; revealing their new supernatural warrior forms.

Ade's clothes begin to change, morphing into a tribal war apparel. He dons a headgear with a pair of huge antlers. His face is disguised with a green leather mask and he is armed with two well adorned axes.

He strikes the two axes and they ignite into flaming weapons, generating the same lighting as Ṣàngó's axes. Ṣàngó is stunned and speechless but as he tries to grasp the young hero's new status, Ade reveals his warrior name, "I am the Warrior Prince" then he levitates into the air. Ṣàngó shouts, "What! You can fly also?" Next Alex's clothes reshapes into a black gothic magician's garment and his hair changes into a slivery wave, blowing in the brewing storm which he generates. His eyes glow and his storm lifts him up high into the air and he hovers above the ground then he announces his warrior name to his team below, "I am Mystic, the Mind Bender".

The two amazed giant deities turn their focus to Makato and ask, "Don't tell us you can fly too.

Without saying a word, a pair of large white wings protrudes from Makato's back and spread, transforming the Samurai into an Angelic being. His wings flap with great strength, blowing a strong wind and causing the two giants to stagger. Makato stretches out his right arm and the flaming Sword from Eden appears in his hand and sizzles with a blue flame; he declares his warrior name to his companions, "I am the Angelic Samurai".

Egbesu shouts aloud, "How the Gaz-elle did you get that? That's the legendary blazing sword of Eden, created by the Almighty Himself!"

Makato flies up to meet his two companions hovering above.

The Oracle and Chief Kabaka begin to sing a native praise song, praying and thanking the Almighty for strengthening His chosen children.

Ṣàngó is still gobsmacked as he watches the three hovering heroes. Egbesu more eager to see what the last hero has in store asks, "And what will you change to, a Ti...?"

Before Egbesu completes his last syllable, Ibi's eyes change to the same bright star-like glow like the other three companions. Her face changes completely, giving her a wild and hypnotic look which is enhanced by an even wilder hair which also changes into dreadlocked weave, embellished with Eagle feathers and native beads. Her skin changes to a camouflage covered with the unmistakable black rosettes spots of the Leopard. Her finger nails grow long, hard and sharp. She is clad in a black woven tribal war garb and she wields a spear which itself radiates some form of energy. A gentle blue aura appears and expands in front of her and a massive ferocious Black Panther steps through the blue mist and gently walks straight to the heroine's side; who herself is already transformed into an unrecognisable warrior. She proclaims her warrior identity, "I am Ẹdụlẹ, the fierce Hunter".

Trying not to betray his amazement, Egbesu asks, "No flight?"

The new Ẹdụlẹ́ does not disappoint the war deity; she generates electrostatic sparks and teleports all around then comes to a rest by Egbesu's side.

Ṣàngó is envious, he fusses, "How come you all can fly and we who have lived for hundreds of years cannot?"

Egbesu pats Ṣàngó on the shoulder and tells him that the four heroes have passed through various trials and have earned the powers that they now possess.

Ade beckons to Ibi to give the call and declare to the enemies that their cover is blown.

CHAPTER 16: WAR OF THE GODS

For God and Mankind

Ibi stands ahead of her advancing companions and facing the unseen enemies she shouts, "Cowardly villains from the dark side show yourselves and receive your judgment. There is no response for a while causing the eight Earth defenders to wonder if the villains will show themselves then they hear a faint roar getting progressively louder as the concealment veil is lifted. The defenders are horror-struck at the swarm of abhorrent devils before their eyes.

Chief Kabaka expresses his shock by commending the valor of Ibi, "Truly, the blood of the Ẹdụlẹ́ runs in your veins. I can't believe this is the horror you beheld and remained so calm; your type of courage has never been seen before".

Ade descends to the ground and turning to Ṣàngó and the company, Ade's speaks with fury in a deep and unusual mature voice, "These are the ones who have caused so many tears in the World and spoken so much lies. They're the ones who have turned brother against brother, Nation against Nation. They are the devils that have constantly tried to separate us from our Father!"

The Warrior Prince leaps forward; beginning the attack. He is followed closely by Ibi, the Ẹdulẹ and her fierce feline, the Black Panther. Alex generates an encircling whirl storm and goes airborne. Makato takes to the air as well, pointing the Blazing sword at his chosen target. His celestial weapon glows even brighter as the sizzling blue flame burns wider, cutting through a line of advancing rabble of Gremlins.
And so the long expected war of the gods begins.

Ṣàngó joins the attack, wielding his double axe, knocking a cluster of enemies far back. The Thunder deity's twin axes spew out bolts of lightning and fire into the advancing devils. Egbesu leaps over the front line of advancing critters into the middle of the battle. The war deity's mace spins like a sharp rotor, cutting several creatures in half at a time.

Chief Kabaka and the old Priestess refuse to be left out of the fight; yelling as they tear into the chaos, they take on the dwarf Gremlins. The stout chief, fortified with protection charms, picks one imp after another and smashes it against another foe. The Oracle conjures a blinding spell, rendering a huge red monster incapacitated, making it easy for the nearby Ẹdulẹ to stab it with her gleaming spear.

The fight rages on uncontrollably; but the number of hell's army continues to grow.

Ade realises that their enemies continue to surge; so he calls out to Ṣàngó, "This is not working; the more we destroy, the more they seem to increase. They are being spawned from underneath us. I think they're trying to keep us busy, buying time for Demonicus to activate the beacon. You and Egbesu go! Stop him, we will take care of things down here!"

Ṣàngó agrees, accepting Ade's order, he responds, "This ends now!"

Ṣàngó signals to Egbesu and points to the red demon on the hill top. The two powerful deities run up the hill, knocking several imps out of their way as they make for the top of the hill.

Alex levitates high above the battle ground and from his vantage position; he warns his comrades, informing them of impending attacks. The airborne Mystic seems to be having fun; he calls the enemies by funny names. He shouts at two tall broad head demon, "Hey, Crab-Heads, look up here!"

The two swaying Mantis looking creatures turn and leap up towards their challenger. Alex cast a mesmerizing spell upon the two wobbling fiends. Both Crab-Heads drop back to the ground and remain immobile, hynotised by the Mystic's trance.

The battle intensifies as more fiends emerge from the pores in the ground creating a multitude of devils pouring upon the gravely outnumbered warriors. Ade's axes cut the imps down like knife cutting through butter, destroying dozens in one sweep. The destroyed devils instantly crumble into a pile of smelly ash and then absorbed by the ground.

Alex alerts Ade, "Hey axe warrior, look behind you, watch out for the ugly serpent!"

The Whisperer swiftly coils around Ade, tightening his serpentine tail around Ade's arms and body. The serpent attempts his fight combo move of burying its victim into the ground up to the neck but his attack strategy is broken by a growl behind. The evil floating coiler is attacked by Ibi's Black Panther who grabs the serpent by its tail, giving Makato some space to swing his Blazing sword and instantly beheading the slimy coiler.

Next Alex yells out a warning to the old Priestess and her fighting companion, Chief Kabaka, "Hey big man, look far ahead, the naked predator has picked you as his target; he charges towards you".

The chief signals the levitating hero, waving to acknowledge his warning. The big man grabs a gremlin by its feet and spins it several times in a circle before throwing the dwarf demon like a lance at the charging naked predator. The Oracle is amused, she nods showing her appreciation for the chief's attack technique.

More teaming creatures swarm the Oracle and Chief Kabaka, who stay close to each other; combining their spells, they generate a blast which throws the entire piling host high into the air and dropping them down like flies and turning into heaps of putrid ash as they are destroyed.

Alex spots a multi-headed monster stalking the Ẹdụlẹ́ hunter. He takes no chance; he alerts his childhood friend, "Ibi, over there, behind you, a Jack and Jill demon stalks you!"

The Ẹdụlẹ́ warrior turns around inquisitively to see what foul creature Alex just described.

Ade's attention is drawn to Ibi when he hears the uncanny cry of the fire breathing beast. He calls to Ibi, "Hold on my dear, I will deal with that abomination".

But an unperturbed Ibi tells her heartthrob warrior, "Don't worry love, I've got this!"

Ibi sees the triple headed monster creeping towards her, ready to pounce on her. The Ẹdụlẹ́ hunter takes a confronting crouching stance, armed with her glowing spear.

It's the Chimera; a terrifying, fast and strong beast, with three heads of unrelated animals, all conjoined to one body. One head is a lion head with feral eyes; a second is a fire breathing goat head and at its rear end is a hissing dragon-head attached to the monster's body by a snake-like tail. The fearsome Chimera is an abhorrent creature spawned by the dark forces of hell. It is said that only a deity can cross its path and live to tell the tale.

The goat head spews a blazing fire at Ibi but the Ẹdụlẹ warrior teleports out of the range of the blaze. Appearing above the beast, she pierces the goat head with her spear, pinning its fire breathing mouth to the ground. She spins around using the spear as a pole and faces the ferocious lion head. The beast's snake tail curves overhead then the dragon head strikes at the preoccupied warrior but the Ẹdụlẹ's Black Panther companion leaps from afar and grabs the dragon head by the neck, biting it clean off from the attaching snake-like tail.

Ade jumps to Ibi's aid and cuts off the lion head. The warrior prince smiles to his darling girl and confesses, "I'm sorry dear, I know you said you didn't need my help but I couldn't bear to see my sweetheart in danger".

Ibi replies to Ade, "I wasn't in any danger but thank you anyway".

She smiles back at her warrior lover and the two lovebirds kiss before going back to their combat mode.

Alex turns around in the air, looking out for any more surprise attacks. He spots another blind charger going for Ade. Alex alerts Ade shouting from the sky, calling to the targeted warrior as if it is all a game, "Hello Ade, Alex calling Ade, red brute Rhino charging head-on, please acknowledge, over".

Ade answers, "Yes, I see it, but why do they charge wildly as if one is just going to stand and be a willing target?"

The blood dripping fiend rams through the battle ground, knocking his own fellow imps out of its way. Ade gets hold of its horns and swings it around, sending it charging back to where it came from.

Meanwhile Makato is at the far end of the battle ground, chasing after a flying bat-like demon all over the sky. Alex calls out to the Samurai angel warrior, "Do you need any help with that screeching bat? It's howling all over the place like an ancient town crier!"

Makato doesn't respond to Alex's playful questions; he is too busy trying to catch the elusive vampire.

Makato remembers the power and characteristics of his Blazing sword. He stops the chase, instead hovers at a spot; then stretching his sword outwards, he lets go of the Blazing sword. Immediately the Blazing sword takes on its natural spinning and encircling mode, zooming at an extreme speed around the battle perimeter. The Vampire demon blinded by the bright flame of the blazing sword flies straight into the path of the divine sword. The arrow-like sword shoots through the flying demon destroying the Vampire. The evil flier turns to ash and drops to the ground.

On the top of the hill, Ṣàngó and Egbesu battle Brutus Demonicus simultaneously on either side forcing the huge demon to stumble backwards. Brutus' pet; the evil hound grabs Ṣàngó foot with its sharp teeth. Ṣàngó shakes the dark canine off and complains to Egbesu, "I hate wild dogs".

Egbesu replies the thunder deity, "Correction, that's not a dog, brother, that's a Wolf; a hound from hell".

In a swift rage, Brutus kicks Egbesu with his huge hoof, almost knocking him off the cliff.

Ṣàngó jumps high up above the red beast and strikes his axes together, generating both fire and lightning then he strikes his enemy; bringing his mighty wrath on the evil foe but the impenetrable wings shield the beast from the thunderous Axes. Demonicus flaps his massive wings, creating a hurricane on the mountain top, sending Ṣàngó and Egbesu tumbling to the ground. Demonicus roars in laughter, "Weak descendants of weak angels. I admire your courage and determination, but like I defeated you once before, here again you will fall and this time, I will destroy you both for good".

Egbesu responds in anger, "How dare you talk of good, you know nothing about goodness and it is you who will fall today!"

Ṣàngó and Egbesu stand up and strike their pairs of Axes together creating a blinding lightning from the sky. They shoot the thunderbolt at their enemy but the mighty Brutus is unscathed. Their powerful adversary is enraged even more. He matches towards the two deities and swings his own colossal sword across his challengers, knocking off their weapons from their hands and throwing the Earth defenders to the ground.

An Unexpected Ally

Demonicus laughs in his trade mark cynical laughter at his fallen challengers; he raises his hellish weapon high up and strikes down as he boasts, "Join your fallen fathers".

His surging sword descends to crush the defenseless pair but it is blocked by a strong steel; creating a blinding light and explosion that sends the huge beast tumbling backwards.

From within the cloud of dust comes a booming laughter; louder even than that of Brutus the beast.

Ṣàngó's expression changes; not looking glad with the new development; decries, "That laughter, I know that laughter".

The dust and flame settles and standing before the two giants lying on the ground is another muscular giant. The newcomer proclaims his own arrival, "Your saviour is here, now let the real battle begin!"

Ṣàngó looks up to the new ally with a frown but Egbesu chuckles and announces their rescuer, "Amadioha! You are most welcome, my brother".

Egbesu then turns to Ṣàngó, "Why the long face, help has come, our number has increased; now let us bring down this foul demon".

Sàngó stands and walks to Amadioha, "I greet you brethren of thunder and lightning; come, fight by my side".

Demonicus recovers and spreads his gargantuan wings making him appear bigger and even more terrifying; then with great fury, the mighty demon charges at the trio with utmost brute force. Amidst the clings and clangs of swords and axes, they battle, creating a frightening rumpus. The melee ends and the brave defenders fall one after the other. The combined strength of the three deities is no match for the demon from hell.

Brutus revels in his victory and mocks the groaning trio then boasts, "Once again you weak children of the so called Watchers have failed. The fifth beacon is ready and the gateway will open for my lord to enter. He will lead us to destroy, once and for all, you pitiable disappointments called the children of God".

The three deities are down and their weapons broken. In a weakening voice, Amadioha apologises to Ṣàngó, "I am sorry for not being by your side all these ages. You and I never stood any chance with the most beautiful daughter of the great Queen Sheba anyway. She had chosen another over us; a common male servant; I guess she was truly looking for love; our contest was in vain".

Egbesu cuts in, "I don't understand you both; here we are fallen and failing in our onerous task to stop evil from taking over this World and you still talk about competing over a girl?"

Ṣàngó reminds Egbesu, "You and I know that we never stood a chance against Brutus Demonicus, mighty captain of Lucifer; it is over. The World will fall. We have failed. The war which began in the high heavens will now be lost here on Earth and we, the last hope of mankind have failed".

Suddenly there is a crashing noise from the battle below. Demonicus looks downhill and sees his numerous demons being defeated by the four young warriors and the collapse of the Devil's head energy post for the Ogoni beacon; being destroyed. He roars, "Noooo!"

Ṣàngó laughs at the weakening evil force and mocks the angry demon, "Well, you are not that unbeatable as you thought. Now tell me, how does it feel to fall at the feet of mere mortals?"

The three fallen defenders laugh at the infuriated monster.

In anger Brutus plunges his huge blade into Ṣàngó's chest, mortally wounding him. He then grabs the thunder deity by the neck and mocks the dying dangling giant, "Let's see you laugh now!"

He throws Ṣàngó from the top of the hill. Ṣàngó falls tumbling over the hard rocky hill and crashes on the ground far below; breaking his back and knocking the ageless deity of thunder out completely. Brutus leaps up in the air and flapping his bloodshot wings, he dives downwards, flying like a ferocious dragon, raging towards the young warriors on the battle ground below.

Beasts of the Five Beacons

Below, on the battle ground, the remaining host of fiends surge towards the indomitable heroes; crowding around the unyielding warriors. Then Alex generates an immense energy then he floats even higher into the air and then with a deafening cry, he unleashes a blast of blinding light, vanquishing the entire horde of devils in the blast pulse.

After the haze of light clears, the battle ground becomes bare, leaving only the four young heroes, Chief Kabaka and the Oracle standing.

Brutus nose-diving at a tremendous speed lands on the ground causing a tremor. He looks around and realising that he is alone, he lets out a shriek; a deafening cry with a resonance that throws the four heroes and their allies backwards, knocking them to the ground.

Then the sky darkens with a thick cloud and four flaming portals appear high up in the sky. There is an immediate apprehension among the Earth's defenders then they see four beastly foes drift through each of the four flaming gateways. They are the four high ranking demons from the other MONKI towns; they have been summoned by their leader, Brutus. They land on the ground with a crashing bang, cracking the ground. Chief Kabaka is worried; he turns to the Oracle; who also is unsure what power the new menacing devils have brought to the war. The big man confesses to the old priestess, "I'm afraid our enemy has regrouped, he has summoned his strongest warring champions".

The Oracle is not intimidated by the arrival of the terrifying demons, she reassures the chief, "Don't worry, he is weakening; so he calls for back-up; that is a sign that he is afraid".

Ade and his three young heroes get up and shake off the sand from their bodies and together they confront the new evil lords.

The four heroes march boldly towards the advancing four demons; Makato recognizes Dagon; the demon who killed and entrapped his parents' souls in his kingdom beneath the Sea; pointing to the tentacle demon, he tells his companions, "Leave this one to me, we have unfinished business".

Makato challenges Dagon, the Demon of the deep.

The other three heroes pick their opponents. Ade faces Beelzebub, the ferocious lord of the flies.

Alex picks Moloch, the brutal winged devil.

Ibi takes on the massive goat-head demon, Chemosh.

Ibi, the wild hunter and shredder, teleports behind Chemosh the abomination, taking her enemy by surprise. The Ẹdụlẹ́ draws first blood, slashing through the hide of the four-horned goat-head demon with her sharp long claws. She buries her claws deep into the devil's hide; he feels the poisonous sting and lets out a high-pitch scream.

The four human heroes engage their opponents in single combat, fighting in the air and on ground until, one by one the generals of the dark World begin to fall. First is Moloch, the harvester of children's souls. He spins wildly in the air towards the air borne Alex who calmly evades the staggering devil. In a swift move, Alex goes behind the clumsy creature and rips his wings off. The demon drops to the ground and disintegrates into a smelly pile of ash.

Seeing his fellow demon destroyed, Chemosh throws his red axe at Ibi but the supernatural hunter teleports away and appears over his head of the demon. Ibi thrusts her glowing celestial spear into the villains head instantly impaling the foul creature; emitting a fetid smell, the destroyed demon crumbles into a pile of ash and is blown away by the wind.

Just then Brutus' black hell hound descends from the hill and leaps fast over rocks towards Ṣàngó, who is already down and broken. With the four heroes full engrossed in their own individual duels with the four powerful hell's generals, Ṣàngó is left helpless. The dark hound goes immediately for Ṣàngó's head but it is intercepted by an equally matched beast, the Black Panther, protector and ally of the Ẹdụlẹ. The agility and strength of the Panther is no match for a mere canine. It grabs the dark hound by the throat and reaps off its head, spilling a foul smelling green slime from the carcass. The Panther then stands guard protecting the thunder deity. Ṣàngó's giant companions, Egbesu and Amadioha; disposed of their weapons; climb down from the hill, and also stand with their dying companion.

Seeing that his favourite pet hound has been ripped apart, Brutus roars in anger and leaps into the air, and flying forward and straight towards the battle below. He lands on the ground and stomps straight towards the Panther. The supernatural feline is immediately flanked by the Oracle and Chief Kabaka, forming a defense line, ready to do battle with the advancing gigantic foe. Chief Kabaka and the old Priestess both combine their spells to create a protective barrier around themselves and three weak deities, but their spells do not hold against the hurricane from the flapping wings of the red monster but Brutus halts his attack on the trio as he sees his four generals falling one after the other.

Makato pierces the flaming sword into the heartless chest of Dagon, the demon of the deep; instantly destroying the creature. Makato breathes a sigh of relief as he utters a statement in Japanese, meaning, "Now all your captives are set free, the spirits of my father and mother can now find rest".
Ade swings his axes across each other in a scissors manner and cuts off the head of Beelzebub and the great beast drops to the ground and instantly dissolves like a blob.

The dead body immediately decomposes into a pile of rotten smelling, soggy ash. Ade moans, holding himself back from puking and remarks, "What a putrid smell!"

Alex agrees with Ade, he complains as well, "That's a huge load of crap, no wonder they call him the lord of the flies".

The four heroes enjoy the humour for a brief moment then prepare for the attack of Brutus Demonicus as he advances without his usual army of fiends.

Ade calls out to Alex, "The beacon, go now, destroy it!"

Alex levitates high to the top of the hill and creates an electrically charged vortex around the main beacon of the MONKI portal. The tower collapses causing the instant disintegration of the other four synced beacons in Mogadishu, N'Djamena, Khartoum and Isiro.

Brutus goes wild and leaps into the midst of the three young warriors and standing alone; he wonders how four young mortals can defeat the powerful army from hell. Surrounded by the young human warriors, he asks arrogantly, "Who the hell are you tiny humans who dare stand against the fearsome might of hell?"

Ade walks up to the forty-foot monster and orders him to vacate the World and go back to the place of torment from where he came.

Brutus asks Ade, "So you are the leader of this gang who oppose the lord of darkness? Then it is you who must die!"

Ade is unfazed by the Brutus' threat, he answers the conceited devil, "I am not the leader; we are companions; and we are the defenders of the World, the mortals who will end your reign of terror on Earth today".

Brutus moves in to kill the young challenger but Ade's three comrades line up with him against the desperate adversary".

A Prophesy Fulfilled

The outnumbered demon pulls out his menacing sword once more and storms his much smaller defiers. Brutus gnashes his ragged teeth in anger; expressing his feeling of humiliation. He swings his massive sword across the attacking line of the daring mortals but they are too fast for the clumsy giant; they evade the huge beast. Ade throws his axes in a curved trail. The twin weapons travel in a boomerang curve, scratching the red monster before returning to the warrior Prince. The Ẹdùlẹ́ teleports behind the groaning enemy, piercing his bat-like membrane wing with her radiating spear further infuriating the demon. Makato distracts the beasts by flying close to his face as he swings wildly at the four encircling antagonists; meanwhile the Mystic hero cast an illusion spell creating many versions of the warriors. The huge enemy roars loudly creating a hurricane which pushes the heroes back.

Even alone, the gigantic demon proves unbeatable. The fighting four close in again and strike at their enemy in one strong coordinated attack but the fierce demon flaps his wide wings repeatedly generating a gale, knocking the airborne warriors to the ground.

Ade remembers the wise words of the Seer at the Monastery in Scotland who charged the heroes to work together and become one weapon but the axe warrior tries to understand how the four can become one weapon. He calls out to Alex, "You are the Mystic; how do we become one force to bring down this beast?"

The Mystic hero shuts his eyes and goes into a trance for a moment, then he opens his eyes and instructs the Samurai angel to touch Ibi's necklace with his Blazing sword. The winged hero flies to Ibi; then standing before the Ẹdùlẹ́, he points his weapon to the heavens. The sword instantly glows even brighter, as if super charged. Then Makato touches Ibi's ancient pendant with the tip of the divine sword. The locket begins to glow with the same bright blue flame of Makato's sword.

The four warriors are astounded; then Alex yells to Ade, "Now what?"
The brief confusion amongst the four comrades gives Brutus just enough time for the beast of hell to gather his strength.

He summons his might, calling to his master in the depths of hell for power. The warriors are further shocked as they see their enemy grow in size right before their eyes and his hellish weapon burst into flames. It is clear that the hemmed enemy is no longer the prey but the predator.

The Oracle calls out to Ade, snapping the dumbfounded hero out of his shock.

Ade is shaken out of the freeze. He drops his twin axes and pulls out his old favoured weapon; the childhood sling; which he always carries with him as a memento.

Ade yells out to Ibi, "Your Pendant, throw it to me!"

Ibi yanks off the necklace and throws it to Ade. He catches the pendant and forces open the sealed locket. He takes out a glowing gem. It is a Turquoise stone, a bluish-green gemstone believed to calm frayed nerves and also one said to connect Heaven and Earth, or can also be used to severe a soul from a spiritual World. The divine stone was given to the first human Ẹdụlẹ́ by the Feline-head Watcher angel and passed on through the line of Ẹdụlẹ́s.

Brutus recognises the gem as the only object that can kill him, both physically and spiritually. He runs towards Ade hoping to snatch the mysterious rock from Ade but the demon halts his attack when he notices a large prehistoric animal walking through a shinny ethereal gate; it is Ade's Lizard King dinosaur friend.

Wasting no time, the Tyrannosaurus Rex sweeps Brutus off his feet with its long tail and the huge demon falls to the ground. The Lizard King roars as if to warn the enemy that he is not done. Brutus tries to quickly recover from the fall but Alex opens a blue portal and his brown dragon friend flies through. The Brown dragon grabs Brutus by the shoulders, lifting the demon slightly off his feet. Brutus struggles so free himself from the gripping claws of the dragon but the flying serpent holds on to its victim like an Eagle holding on to its catch but the champion of hell is no ordinary foe, he bites the brown dragon on its foot causing it to let go.

Demonicus breaks free and scoffs at the young warriors, "You babies think you can defeat me when even your heavenly guardians and their Nephilim descendants have failed?"

The furious beast matches towards Ade; advancing for a determined kill; but the brave warrior remains calm; he stares at the old wooden sling and whispers to it, "My dependable friend, you never missed before, please don't fail me now".

He raises the sling and aims his childhood weapon at the advancing enemy. He lets go his sling and his missile finds its target, the broad forehead of Brutus.

For a moment all went quiet; Demonicus stands still and in absolute shock, looking around as if wondering what just happened. Then with a final look up to the crumbling beacon on the top of the hill, the mighty champion of hell drops to the ground.

Makato immediately flies to the fallen Monster and in a swift move swings his Blazing sword and cuts off the head of Brutus Demonicus who is also known as Belial. Like all his fallen devils, Brutus decomposes into a huge pile of foul smelling ash.

The oracle raises her hands to the heavens, dancing and singing praises to God. The old Priestess then recalls the story of David, the young boy; an underdog who slew the Philistine warrior giant, Goliath and eventually became the King. She then breathes a sigh of relief and declares, "The prophesy has been fulfilled".

Makato flies to where Sàngó is lying, frail and dying, flanked by his two compatriots, Egbesu and Amadioha. The Samurai angel wraps the fading deity with his Angelic wings; like the Guardian angel did to him at the forbidden forest. Makato's wings begin to glow and pulsate. The Samurai angel unfurls his wings and Sàngó is seen smiling, his wounds completely healed and his full strength recovered, he gets up and stretches as if he has been asleep all this while. Makato also heals the other two severely wounded deities; everyone jubilates then Egbesu and Amadioha bow to the new keeper of the Blazing Sword.

A Sad Departure

Sàngó calls the four heroes together and gives them one final task. He tells them, "Listen very carefully; our enemy, Brutus Demonicus is defeated and the five beacons have collapsed but the dangerous institutions they control around the World are still in operation. Their headquarters in England must be dismantled and their leaders must be exposed".

Egbesu walks up to his protégé, Makato; the war deity and the Samurai angel clink their weapons together as a gesture of mutual respect. Makato asks the giant warrior if he can touch the deity's legendary weapon but Egbesu tells him that there is no weapon ever made that is more powerful than the one which he, Makato already possesses. Then the two great warriors bow to each other.

The fierce Black Panther trots up to Ibi and licks her hand. The Ẹdụlẹ́ warrior leans slightly over and rubs her forehead on the soft black fur on the forehead of her feline companion. The huge animal turns around and leaps away; disappearing into thin air.

Ade likewise, gives a big hug to his prehistoric ally. The gigantic dinosaur roars to acknowledge Ade's gesture; then the Lizard King walks into a large portal and disappears.

Alex's dragon pal circles overhead; he does an acrobatic spin which is appreciated with cheers from the group of warriors below and then it flies away towards the woods.

Sàngó bends over to Ade and slaps his large hand unto the small hand of his tribe's man, producing a loud high five. Ade becomes emotional and sad that the individual who brought all this mission to pass and with whom he has become very fund of will final be gone forever. Sàngó raises his twin axes and Ade does the same with his. The two wielders of thunder and lightning then strike their weapons together, causing a light spark. Still emotional Ade hugs the giant deity very tight, holding on to his mentor for some time. Ibi runs to the embracing pair and wraps her arms around the two. Everyone is saddened by the realization that the three deities will soon depart, never to be seen again.

Chief Kabaka bows to the three giants then he turns to Egbesu; whose shrine he has guarded almost all his life; he asks for a souvenir from the war deity, something he can continue to preserve and guard for the rest of his life. The war deity hands over his mace to the chief. The huge weapon is too heavy for the chief; he falls backwards to the ground but saves his new treasured object from touching the ground. The Chief shouts, "I saved it!"

Everyone laughs then slowly the happy moment fades into a solemn mood and then they all move about; embracing one another, for a final farewell. The giants separate themselves from the others, ready to be transported away from their presence. Amadioha then recites the same verse which the four heroes have heard before, "Long ago, mankind knew the powers that he inherited from the creator. There was a time when the seas were calm and the sky was clear; but the rulers of men put their individual interests before the happiness of the people. Elders grew thirsty with lust for knowledge without wisdom. Kings sought power without compassion; and so the World lost its soul, then evil became bold and ruled where men once did. It is in the children that the World must once again find its courage. Children who once before and has again defeated giants".

He concludes as he points at the heroes, "The time has now come when you, the children of man must rediscover the power within, and become whom you were born to be".

Ṣàngó, Egbesu and Amadioha bid the four heroes, Chief Kabaka and the Oracle farewell; formally announcing their departure, "Now that the enemy has been destroyed and evil vanquished; we, the descendants of the Nephilim can now ascend to the realm of God and finally rest and be at peace".

Ade tries one last appeal to Ṣàngó, hoping to stop the deities' transfiguration. Ibi also lends her voice, asking Egbesu to reconsider their departure; pleading that the strengths of the giants are much needed to defend the World if ever the dark side should return but Amadioha assures the new heroes that their strengths and weapons are more than the World needs to protect mankind. The three giant warriors are not persuaded from leaving; they simply smile, then looking up to the heavens they recite their praise to the Almighty, "For the kingdom, the power and the glory are yours, now and forever".

They slowly ascend high into the sky and fade.

The Oracle tells the new defenders of the World that they will be most welcome to remain in Ogoniland; Makato chooses to stay but Ade tells Ibi and Alex to go on back home to England while he travels to Óké-Ífẹ̀ to look for his mother. Alex and Ibi insist they will not be parted from Ade; not after going through all what they endured and survived together, insisting that they now stand as one family; and Ibi adds that she's not about to be parted from her love again. The four warriors transform back to their mortal forms and Makato takes his three companions back across the sea and to the airport in Port-Harcourt for a charter flight to Óké-Ífẹ̀.

CHAPTER 17: A NEW BEGINNING

Ade Returns to Óké-Ífè

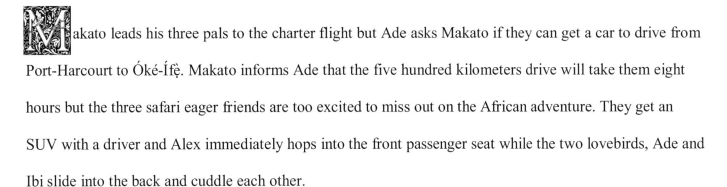akato leads his three pals to the charter flight but Ade asks Makato if they can get a car to drive from Port-Harcourt to Óké-Ífè. Makato informs Ade that the five hundred kilometers drive will take them eight hours but the three safari eager friends are too excited to miss out on the African adventure. They get an SUV with a driver and Alex immediately hops into the front passenger seat while the two lovebirds, Ade and Ibi slide into the back and cuddle each other.

Alex teases Ade, "Hey Warrior Prince, what will you do if Ibi finds a more handsome dude when we get to your town? Will you transform and chop of his head?"

Ade responds cynically, "I will transform alright but it will be your head, I will chop off because you must have cast a spell to put it into his head because my love only has eyes for me".

Ibi is flattered but reminds the two men that their powers won't work against each other since they get their authority from the same source.

The happy friends crack personal jokes and laugh as they drive through the lonely Country road. The eight hour drive passes quickly and the fun comes to an end when Ade sees the welcome road sign at the old stone arch-way into Óké-Ífè. His countenance changes immediately as they drive into the ancient town; his cheerful disposition soon fades into a sombre mood.

Ibi holds his hand and asks if he is okay but Ade doesn't respond, his eyes is fixated on an old crumbling church building. Then with tears in his eyes, he points to the church and tells his two companions that the old church is the same one where he and his mother took refuge when they escaped the hunt from the palace thugs. His head turns around, still fixed on the building even as the car drives pass it. He tells his friends that it was in the church he met his adopted parent, who raised him to become the man he is now.

Ibi quickly adds, "And to them, I am grateful because I owe my meeting you to them".

Ade kisses Ibi on her lips, reciprocating her proclamation of love.

The road to Ade's old house is no longer there; new modern buildings are seen everywhere and the population of people also is no longer what is was; there are so many schools and multi-storey houses built along the road. Then Ade tells the driver to stop to ask for directions then they drive slowly off the main highway onto a dirt road. They eventually find Ade's old house but it is abandoned and broken down. They come down from the car and walk along the narrow path to the Palace. No one recognises the Prince and he too does not find a familiar face. Ade asks to meet the King but he is told that there is no King but a Baálẹ̀; the traditional lesser ruler of the Kingdom. Ade and his friends are taken into the Palace council chamber where they are welcome to seat down. Not long, an old man dressed in regal flowing Yoruba Àgbàdà attire enters to meet the strangers. He immediately recognises Ade; jumping up and running to hug Ade, he shouts so loud, "Adebọ̀wàlé, the crown has come back home!" A crowd of Palace chiefs begins to gather in the chamber and in the midst of the commotion, Ade takes a closer look at the old man, then he recognises the Baálẹ̀ as the same one who protected him, when he was being hunted as a child and also his father's most trusted ally who had tried to save his father from the wicked traitors of the Palace.

The Baálẹ̀ announces to the gathering; singing and reciting praises that the lost Prince has returned. Everyone rejoices and the royal drummers are brought in to further spread the good news beyond the walls of the chamber. There is much celebration but Ade's heart is heavy for he still has not heard about his mother.

The Baálẹ̀ walks with Ade into the garden; first he assures the worried Prince that his mother is alive and well and he will be taken to her. He then narrates to Ade that after Ade's father was killed in the palace; he, the Baálẹ̀ was banished from the town for fear of him raising a rebellion against the rogue new King. Then he tells Ade that there was a famine, accompanied by strange diseases. People began to die, so the Oracle was consulted and it was revealed that the spilling of the innocent blood of Ade's father angered the gods which caused the pestilence. The people revolted and drove the King and his cohorts away from the Palace and out of the town. The Palace priest offered several offerings to appease the gods but things only got a little better.

While the sickness and deaths reduced, the famine continued and so it has remained over the years.

The people brought him back as the Baálẹ̀, to be a caretaker until a King is crowned.

When he came back, he looked for Ade's mother all around the town and nearby villages then she was found living in an abandoned shed near the market, for she was also banished by the wicked King. The young men of the town came together and built a house for Ade's mother on a piece of land which he, the Baálẹ̀ gave to her.

After the gloomy tale, the Baálẹ̀ then gets a Palace messenger to take Ade and his friends to Ade's mother. They drive to a nearby village where they see Ade's mother far off in her farm tending her crops. Ibi and Alex wait by the car while Ade walks into the garden towards the aging woman. Ade calls out to her in his old boyish way, "Màámi!"

She recognises the voice but remains frozen in disbelief, still backing the approaching footsteps. Then Ade touches her by the shoulder and gently turns her around. The old woman falls to her knees crying and Ade lifts her up back to her feet. They hold each other in a prolong embrace consoling each other and thanking God for keeping their love one alive. Ade walks his mother back to the car to meet his friends. His mother greets Alex and pulls Ibi near and tells her that she can see in her eyes, the glow of love in them. Ade holds his two precious women in both hands and formally introduces Ibi to his mother. Ibi kneels before Ade's mother and the happy mother quickly lifts the young lady up, welcoming her into the family.

Ade's mother and Ibi both go into the kitchen and prepare a delicious meal for everyone.

Ade and his mother share their joyful reunion with his best friends, recalling happy childhood memories, singing and dancing trying to make up for the long missed years.

The next day, the elders' council prepare to crown their returned Prince as their new King which they believe will bring closure to the sad past and usher in a new era of prosperity to the Kingdom; but Ade requests that the ceremony be put on hold so that he can go visit his adopted parents in London and also to conclude an unfinished task; the secret mission of ridding the World of the remnants of the dark World.

He also implores his uncle the Baálẹ̀ to continue his role of running the Kingdom until after the coronation, but the elders refused, insisting that it is the will of the gods for a new King to ascend the throne, that is why the god have brought him back to them.

Ibi and Alex convinces their friend to do the wish of his people, agreeing with the elders that leaving the King's throne unoccupied any longer, is dangerous, for a society without a head is as bad as one with a bad leader.

The coronation starts the same day with a series of traditional cleansing rituals, purifying the Prince and a procession around the town, presenting the new monarch to the people. Long trumpets sound the news of a new King in the community.

Back at the palace, Ade completes more rituals and ceremonies and is given an elaborately adorned wooden staff symbolising his authority of office, formally making him the new King.

Alex is clad in a princely garment while Ibi is dressed in an intricately decorated princess dress with a delicate weave of beads twisted into her natural long and shiny hair; they are both given seats on Ade's left side; with Ibi, seating next to the new King.

Ade's mother is given the revered royal bronze stool on the right side of the King; she is conferred with the royal title of Yeye Oba; that is the Queen Mother; a formal advisory position.

There is merriment in and around the Palace all day and night. The new King spends the next couple of days organizing his cabinet of Chiefs and tasking them with important duties.

A week after the coronation, Ade, Ibi and Alex prepare to return to England to their families. Ade hands over his staff of office to the trusted Baálẹ̀; giving him the authority of custodian of the Throne and making him a provisional ruler over the Kingdom until Ade's return.

Ade's mother relocates to the palace, where she is cared for and treated with the royalty that comes with her new status of Queen Mother.

As Ade and his friends drive off from the Palace to the airport, Alex tells the new King, "You're no longer the Warrior Prince; now you are a warrior and a King; so from now on you'll be called The Warrior King".

It is not The End

The three heroes return to London after the extensive colourful celebrations in Óké-Ífẹ̀. The airport taxi drops them at Vintage Street and as usual, the Dark Shade gang is seen loitering around. The three returnees are quickly spotted by one of the rascals and he immediately calls the attention of his gang boys. They tease the three friends as they alight from the taxi but the three anxious companions are too eager to find their parents. They run into their individual houses to check on their loved ones.

Alex finds his dad at home, lying on his comfort rocking chair, dozing; his face covered by the voluminous book he must have been reading. The superhero son, gently floats around to the back of the chair and smiles in relief seeing that his father is back home well; unlike the last time he saw his dad being taken into an ambulance. Prof Rosi wakes up sensing that someone entered his house. He finds his son in the room, standing behind the couch, smiling. The old man wipes his eyes to be sure that he is not dreaming. Alex does not wait for his father to confirm his reality; he rams into his dad with a tight hug, almost knocking the old man down on the rug. He kisses the sober old man on his forehead and asks, "How are you dad?"

There is no reply from the dad, just a continuous embrace.

Ade's adopted parents are too happy to see their usually stern-face son back home that they do not bother to ask where he has been but they are surprised when Ade jumps in between the two of them and tells them, "I have a lot to tell you two".

Ade's mom forces the excited young man to sit still while she hurries into the kitchen to get him something to drink.

Before Ade's dad can utter a word, Ade tells him, "I have been in Africa!"

He continues, "I can't tell you everything but; I met my mother".

His eyes catches his mom's who is walking out of the kitchen with a glass of cold orange juice and then the embarrassed son rephrases his words, "I met my biological mother; you know, the one who gave me to you!"

The old couple are astounded and don't know what to say but the over excited Ade continues, "I wasn't alone; Ibi and Alex were with me. We were sent on an urgent errand. I'm sorry there was no time to tell you; but don't worry, I will tell you everything!"

Ade pauses again then corrects himself, "Well, maybe not everything but …"

He ignores his parents and peeps through the window and tells them; rushing back outside, "I have to see Ibi. I love you both!"

The reverends are just glad that their son is safe and home, they shrug their shoulders and Rev. Brown takes the glass of juice from his wife for himself and continues watching the TV.

Inside Ibi's house, her dad runs towards his missing daughter as she enters the house and lifts her up, almost knocking her head on the ceiling. He inspects the calm young lady all over as he asks, "Are you okay. Are you hurt? Where have you been?

Ibi allows her father to finish his interrogation before she answers, "I was only gone for a few weeks; now you know how I always feel when you go for months".

Her father apologises and promises never to leave her alone again, vowing to resign from the overseas job and instead get a job in England.

Ibi changes the mood, "Now that we have that out of the way, I will tell you an unbelievable story but first, I must go out briefly to check on my boyfriend".

Mr. Smith is taken aback, not knowing whether to be protective or scold his daughter for being so casual about having a boyfriend he doesn't know.

She leans out of the entrance door and waves to Ade, who is walking towards her house, she then turns to her father and prepares him for another shocker, "Don't worry, you'll meet him now".

After meeting Ibi's father and answering his unending questions, Ade is finally let off the hook. Ibi finds it amusing that the tough Warrior King is intimidated by just one simple man, she takes Ade's hand and they both walk along their street with several eyes staring and tongues wagging. The girls whisper and murmur, gossiping as the couple strolls along the street. The Dark Shade boss, Chris crosses the couples' path and stops the happy lover boy from passing. Ade is not bothered but Ibi will have none of the rascal's harassment. She grabs the bully's arm and in a flash, she extends her sharp Panther claws and scratches the macho man's arm, injecting venom into the gang leader. Chris lets out a scream as he feels the sharp sting then everyone notices that the Street's strong man has peed himself.

His thugs gape with embarrassment and offer their coats to shield their boss's wet pants but he is too humiliated; he runs inside his house and locks himself inside. The girls of Vintage Street all laugh at the supposed terror of the neighbourhood.

Alex meets the crowd laughing in the middle of the street; he joins in the mockery but reminds his mates that they still have a mission to complete.

Ade agrees and asks his fellow warriors, "Are you two ready to kick some old ghoulish butt?"

Ibi replies, "We need a ride". Then kissing Ade on the cheeks, she adds cynically, "Not that yellow Mini, you got us into the last time, honey".

The three unwavering heroes nod; then Alex reassures Ade and Ibi, "I think I can manage to teleport three of us over such a short distance".

They walk into a narrow alley and hold hands; with Alex in the middle then the Mystic does his vortex thing and they are immediately sucked into the whirlpool and taken up into the sky, vanishing as they ascend.

The three heroes appear in front of the meeting lodge in their full warrior regalia. They find that the secret meeting place of the dark order has been abandoned. Ade and Ibi go in through the front entrance while Alex circles round the old English mansion midair. Ade is worried; he takes responsibility for their failure saying, "It's my fault, I made us waste too much time at my home town".

Ibi calms the Warrior King, telling her companions, "Let the cowards hide for now. We will be waiting for them whenever they show up again".

Alex transports the team back to the alleyway and the young heroes wonder what hope there is for mankind against such powerful evil force.

Ade reminds his friends that it is not just a question of protecting the World against demons and evil creatures from hell but that the children and youngsters all around the World need proper enlightenment and mentoring so that they will not be easily led by the human disciples of hell; who constantly come up with various evil plans to corrupt the minds of the people; preparing the World to accept the foul ways of the enemy, so that when their master eventually reveals himself, his doctrines of demons will be easily welcome in the World.

On the other hand, Alex reminds his friends how they set out at the beginning of the mission, also naïve and unprepared for what lay ahead of them, but somehow, they did not only survive the impossible, they defeated the five powerful commanders of hell. He adds that so will others who will come after them, learn as they grow. He concludes by saying, "Darkness will always succumb to light because with God, all things are possible".

The three heroes stroll back to their respective homes, hopeful that all will be well.

And so, for many years, there was peace across the World; until...

... NOT THE END

Long ago, mankind ... the powers that h... ...ited from the creator. ... a time when the seas ... calm and the sky was ...ar; but the rulers of men ... their individual intere... before the happiness ... people.

Elders grew thirsty with lust for knowle... without wisdom. Kings sought pow... ...ut compassion; and so the World lost ... ther... evil became bold and ruled where men once did.

It is in the children that we must once a... find our courage. Children who once defe... giants; and young men fought and tamed ... lions.

The time has ... ome ... the children man mu... ...dis... ... within. ... become wh... ... w... ... be...

Printed in Great Britain
by Amazon